THE SOLITUDE OF A SHADOW

Praise for *The Solitude of a Shadow*

'Small-town India comes alive with menace in this taut, hypnotic novel of humiliation and revenge. N. Kalyan Raman's translation is a pleasure to read.'

– AMITABHA BAGCHI

'Devibharathi tells a complex story of love and revenge in a crisp, nuanced language. N. Kalyan Raman's exquisite translation matches his literary craft, marked by its simplicity as well as the slow rise in tempo. A compelling read.'

– JAYASREE KALATHIL

THE SOLITUDE OF A SHADOW

devibharathi

TRANSLATED FROM THE TAMIL BY N. KALYAN RAMAN

HARPERPERENNIAL

An Imprint of HarperCollins *Publishers*

First published in English in India by Harper Perennial 2024
An imprint of HarperCollins *Publishers*
4th Floor, Tower A, Building No. 10, DLF Cyber City,
DLF Phase II, Gurugram, Haryana – 122002
www.harpercollins.co.in

2 4 6 8 10 9 7 5 3 1

Originally published in Tamil as *Nizhalin Thanimai*
by Kalachuvadu Publications, Nagercoil

P-ISBN: 978-93-5489-955-3
E-ISBN: 978-93-5489-976-8

Typeset in 11.5/16.2 Adobe Caslon Pro at
Manipal Technologies Limited, Manipal

Printed and bound at
Replika Press Pvt. Ltd.

FSC
www.fsc.org
MIX
Paper from
responsible sources
FSC® C016779

This book is produced from independently certified FSC® paper to ensure responsible forest management.

For Pudumaipithan,
pioneer of Tamil modernist literature

KARUNAKARAN HAD TURNED UP BEFORE us like an evil spirit after nearly thirty years.

Condemned to a life of flitting constantly like an imp between good and evil, I had joined as a clerk in that government high school only two days ago. With its facade painted a dull yellow, the school stood on a desolate plot on the outskirts of that small town. The previous clerk had been suspended for embezzling public funds and I had taken charge in his place. The headmaster treated me with utmost caution. He asked me why I wanted to move from the powerful district education office in the capital to this rural school which held no prospect of extra income. When I told him I had no taste for big-city life, he refused to believe me. He might have thought that I was being evasive.

Like a spectral beast, the dark shadow of suspicion emerged silently from his ash-grey eyes and began to claw at me with its disgusting paws. Since I had a thick skin that made me impervious to such attacks, I chose to ignore it. After submitting my joining report, I went over to the rickety wooden chair meant for the clerk. It had been vacant for more than six months, and now it was mine.

I introduced myself courteously to everyone who drifted into view—office colleagues and teachers for the most part. Since I was going to work as a close aide to the headmaster, a man who had authority over them, their surreptitious glances, signalling at once the intimacy of friendship and the distance of enmity, began to surround me.

Meanwhile, the headmaster had called for me. I abandoned the physical education teacher who had just introduced himself to me and started a conversation, and came out of the wooden cubicle that separated me and the headmaster. It was then that I saw the ghoulish figure of Karunakaran. The man who had occupied my vengeful heart for thirty years as the epitome of evil was there in front of me in flesh and blood. I felt disoriented for a moment. Then I remembered my sister Sharada's brown eyes wandering endlessly like mine in an unfulfilled quest for revenge.

Even before Karunakaran's name was squeezed out from my lips reluctantly like toothpaste and released into the room, Sharada had become edgy. Her body was trembling. I was afraid that she might, as happened so often in the movies, drop the coffee cup from her hand, and it might crash to the floor and shatter into pieces. But she did not lose her composure right away. She might have waited for him with the confident expectation that this meeting would happen someday. The smouldering embers of her vengeance had begun to shed the layers of ash deposited by time.

'When and where did you see him?'

We sat facing each other in her living room like frogs emerging from their hidey-holes in the rainy season. Her husband was not home yet. Her son, a first-year engineering student, was playing cricket in a park close by. A mega serial with a former celebrity as the female lead was playing on the television. I had mentioned Karunakaran's name in a low whisper during a commercial break.

As the mother of two grown children, exhausted from grappling with a life besieged by misfortune, Sharada harboured secret dreams of fulfilling what remained of her filial duties and living out her old age in peace. Raised under her strict supervision, her children had earned a reputation as responsible youngsters. Being extremely frugal with money, she had been able to marry her daughter off into a respectable family and get her son admitted to an engineering college. She had also sold off her jewellery and taken a loan from the bank to build an elegant and compact house for her family.

When I fell sick a year ago, I went through a phase of loitering around aimlessly. But since I did not wish to seek anyone's sympathy, I stopped visiting Sharada. During my rare visits to her house in deference to insistent invitations from Sharada and her guileless husband, I would sit in a chair in the hall like a stranger and leave early. I would remind myself that there was no consolation to be had from her hospitality and attention. I knew it would be no easy task to remind a kind and mature woman like Sharada about a man like Karunakaran.

Sharada interrupted me fretfully as I described the circumstances in which I had met Karunakaran. It was not difficult for me to guess that a plan was taking swift shape in her mind. While she appeared to be calm initially, she became increasingly distraught—far more than I would have expected. Shutting and bolting the back door, she walked silently towards me. Though carrying the weight of her obese body was already becoming difficult for her, she reached the hall in quick strides. She lowered her voice until it was nearly inaudible. Then, without beating about the bush, she came straight to the point.

Reminding me of the vow I had taken thirty years ago to wreak vengeance on Karunakaran, she said that time had given us a miraculous opportunity to fulfil that vow.

'It's destiny that has brought you to where he is,' she said, her voice cracking with emotion.

In a smoke-filled room above the post office that was housed in a rundown building in the small town where we lived thirty years ago, Karunakaran had been introduced to us as the kind owner of a loan shop. Now, as I waited like a foot servant on the same man who was used to ruining the lives of those trapped in his ruthless grip, Sharada's ambition seemed pitiful to me.

I recognized him at first glance. Noticing the sudden stiffness in my bearing, the headmaster became perturbed. There was no major change in Karunakaran's appearance. His moustache had greyed. His hairline had receded. He wore a pair of gold-framed spectacles. He was dressed in pure white handloom clothes. He appeared to be an important and respected man in that small town. I had just finished signing the attendance register when I saw the headmaster greet Karunakaran with folded hands and lead him to his seat deferentially. To avoid being seen by him, I lowered my head like a tortoise and slid back in my chair.

I don't know how to explain what happened next. Teachers arrived in groups and stood in the headmaster's room. The same fawning attitude was evident in their body language. After making polite inquiries to each group, Karunakaran listened with sympathy and condescension to their complaints about the quality of students' education, the condition of the classrooms and some basic facilities that were yet to be provided, along with their personal grievances.

'I am going to Madras this week. I've already briefed the minister. "No big deal, maapla. Who am I going to look after if not the folks in our school?" he said to me. In any case, prepare a report and give it to the clerk by this evening. Has the clerk joined? The district education officer had assured me that he would fill the position last week.' Only when I heard what he was saying to those standing around him did I begin to remember my childhood vow, one that I had given up long ago as a juvenile fantasy and an impossible dream.

Then the headmaster called me. Though I could hear him clearly, I sat paralysed in my chair. He became incensed. Since it had barely been an hour since I had joined, it was quite likely that his brain had not registered my name. He called out for me using different terms—such as 'Sir' and 'Clerk Sir'—and, unable to bear the insult, summoned the school's night watchman, who was standing outside the door, by his name. Realizing that the situation could take a disastrous turn, the night watchman approached me, placed a hand on my numb shoulder and whispered, 'Sir, HM is calling you.'

As she listened to this story, Sharada became as still as an embalmed cadaver. Already lost in a desert of helplessness, I watched the colourless and odourless apparition of hope leave her obese body and melt into the night.

Then it was time for her husband to return from office. Sharada surfaced abruptly from her reverie and got up. Leaving the front door ajar, she went to the bathroom to wash her haggard face. Just then her husband entered the house. In that agitated state, my face must have looked grotesque. By pretending to watch the news on television, which was playing at a low volume, I managed to keep my face away from his line of sight.

'When did you come?' he said; then, taking the remote from my hand, he raised the volume and, as if by involuntary reflex, kept switching channels as he chatted with me. Since I had nothing new to tell him, he got up quite soon.

'Sharada! Sharada!' Calling out to her for no apparent reason, he went to the bedroom. Then he came back, with a lungi wrapped around his waist. 'Is your mother all right?' he asked and, without waiting for an answer, he shouted towards the kitchen, 'Sharada, did you give him coffee?'

When Sharada came in with the coffee cups, her face was clouded by anxiety about the residual issues of the day. Without faltering even for a moment, she told her husband about the visitor who had come to see him that morning and the message that he had conveyed. As she began reciting a litany of complaints about their son's irresponsible behaviour, she even sounded happy.

'The boy left home this morning and he still isn't back. He plays cricket all the time. He doesn't even eat his lunch properly. When I ask him why he is hurrying, he says lunch break is only for ten minutes. Doesn't touch his books at all. Just you wait. Very soon he is going to earn crores and crores like Sachin and bring it all home.'

'He is a bowler, di. A spinner like Kumble and Murali.'

'What is a spinner?'

Even as he was responding to her, he proceeded to leave the room. Noting that her house had returned to its normal state, I got up with a sigh. 'Why don't you stay back and leave in the morning?' he said to me, but without waiting for a reply, he called his wife. She pushed a tiffin-box that was packed and ready into my hands. 'What is in it?' I asked her. Without a word, she walked me to the door.

I started my ancient Bajaj M-80 moped with a mighty kick and was about to take my leave when she came up to me and stood with her hands resting on the handlebar. 'How many times have I told you to get rid of this piece of junk and buy a new vehicle?' Asking me the same question that she did every time I was about to leave, she looked deep into my eyes. I tried to avoid getting caught in the mysterious grip of her brown eyes.

'All right. I'll be going.'

'Give me a ring tomorrow.' The hint of insistence in her raspy voice, bereft of its usual gentleness, was unnerving to me.

Beating the menacing traffic on the highway, my M-80 carried me slowly along village roads humming with the bustle of birds and countless small animals. Still haunted by memories of the past, I stopped at an abandoned temple by the roadside. Sitting amidst the dry brown remnants of neem flowers scattered on its broken pyol, I lit a cigarette.

I wondered what extraordinary feat an indigent clerk could possibly accomplish when he lacked the means to even replace a useless, obsolete vehicle, and had to support an aged mother and a sister abandoned by her husband.

I was unable to decide whether fate, which had exhumed Karunakaran's stinking body from the death-pit of memory and laid him within arm's reach, wanted to challenge or mock me.

By then, I had no recollection at all of what I had told that man with the poison fangs and forked tongue as he watched me from inside his coiled body ensconced in the headmaster's chair, or what he had asked me. The headmaster had apologized to him for my behaviour perhaps. I was staring intently at his face then. I had no doubt that the angle at which I was standing afforded him a clear view of my face. I wanted to remind him of the face I had thirty years ago and of the scrawny weakling who had stood before him holding a sickle in his raised hand.

When the shadow of suspicion in Karunakaran's eyes began to shift, the assistant headmaster's hands gripped my shoulder. 'He is not feeling well, it seems.' Saying this in an apologetic tone, the assistant headmaster led me away, supporting me on his arm gently. Stretched out on the long table that took up more than half the space in the staff room, I pretended to have fainted, closed my eyes and drew my eyeballs deep inside their sockets. The desire for wreaking vengeance on Karunakaran had begun to fill my heart with its sludge. The embalmed body of that unfortunate day loomed over us like a curse and the repulsive pustules of its memory were floating in that sludge.

Amma, who was a witness, never recalled that ill-fated day again. I suspected that she might have been a secret enabler too. She might have thought that a twelve-year-old boy couldn't have understood anything. Concealing the incident from Appa must have been her main worry at the time. It had not even occurred to her to put her arms around her daughter who was lying there devastated. With the free end of her sari, she dabbed away the blood that had trickled from the nail marks on Sharada's bare breasts, which looked like a pair of upturned chrysanthemums; then she hastened to clasp the hooks on Sharada's torn blouse and cover her chest with her half-sari.

Whenever I happened to recall the incident later, I thought that what she had said—'It's nothing. You'll be all right'—was meant more to pacify Sharada than console her.

As we were leaving, Karunakaran held out a five-rupee note to Amma. I watched them with shock and outrage, almost unable to bear it. I imagined her refusing to accept it, tearing it up and throwing the pieces on his arrogant face, cursing him for his brute nature as she left the room with both of us in tow.

Having lost the sickle in my hand to Karunakaran, I had vowed revenge just before she arrived: 'No matter how long it takes, I won't rest until I have chopped you to pieces one day. I'll avenge this, da.' I have not forgotten how, as I said this theatrically in my childish, still feminine voice, facing him directly, a forlorn smile had appeared on

Sharada's face. I can't say with certainty whether 'I'll avenge this' was part of the statement or I had imagined it later to suit my understanding of the situation.

Similarly, I have no recollection now of whether Amma took his leave when she left.

Amma arrived at the loan shop right after I had made my vow. Listening to my outburst, Karunakaran had started laughing uproariously. Sharada was watching everyone with eyes that had run dry of tears. The moment she saw Amma, as though she believed that Amma would punish him for what he had done to her, Sharada started wailing and crying. As we were going down the stairs, he said with a disgusting smirk, 'The boy watches a lot of movies, it seems. Such a small runt. You are no bigger than a crab, but you stood there with a sickle in your hand and threatened to kill me.'

I sat by Amma's bedside for many days, hoping for at least one word between her sickbed laments that would offer a clue as to whether she remembered even a bit of that grotesque day. I couldn't believe that she might have erased it completely from her consciousness. Burning with the desire to tell Amma about my encounter with Karunakaran and stoke memories of the past in her decrepit brain, I bade goodbye to the disfigured idols of the vengeful deities in that dilapidated temple and set out for home.

Amma's condition seemed much worse than it had been in the morning. My frightened younger sister had arranged for a home visit by a doctor from a small clinic in a nearby town. When I entered, my sister was removing Amma's urine-drenched clothes from her inert body. Averse to seeing the naked body of an old, ailing woman, the doctor turned away and stood facing the wall. Then, as though he had finally made up his mind, he let out a deep sigh and asked several questions of my mother and sister. I remained silent for the most part.

After the doctor left, I sat on the edge of the bed looking at my mother's face. The odour of death that was leaking from every pore in her body was turning me into a monster. The potency of the drug injected into her for temporary relief had dragged her into the dark oblivion of sleep.

Exactly three days later, I had the good fortune of meeting Karunakaran. I had to get a few signatures from him in his capacity as the president of the school's Parent-Teacher Association. It was one of my routine tasks as the school clerk. Armed with the necessary files and register, I stood before the headmaster in his room to get his permission. He appeared tense as always. Taking the files from me, he scrutinized them with great care. After confirming that I had collected all the necessary documents, he told me in a tone of admonition that Karunakaran was a busy man, and that I should wait for him patiently.

Then he motioned me to come a little closer. Lowering his voice as if confiding a secret, he gave me elaborate instructions on how I should conduct myself. He was afraid that I might be rude and disrespectful. 'You may not know it, Sir. You are new here. He has done a lot for this school. He is not really interested in this position and everything that comes with it. But we insisted that he should take this up. Look, so many buildings! There are many government schools where they are still holding classes under a tree. We have four surplus classrooms. We have converted one of those into our staff room. All this happened thanks to his initiative and effort. On a personal level, he is a very good man. Anyone who needs his help can approach him without hesitation. Truly a fine gentleman. The other day, you had taken ill suddenly. Even I was angry that you were standing stock-still without saying anything. But he was not in the least upset. He asked us to take you to a hospital first...' By now the number of people caught in the vice-like grip of his kindness must have increased to a frightening extent, I thought.

To avoid disturbing others with the noise from my M-80, I parked it in the shade of a neem tree in front of Karunakaran's house and went inside. The aura of that old mansion—it looked like a zamindar's dilapidated bungalow surrounded by crotons and many strange trees that seemed out of place—made me nervous. Several people had gathered in front of the house, but a fearsome silence prevailed, as though the place was completely deserted. Poor supplicants whose emaciated bodies gave off an unpleasant odour of sweat waited in the hall in the front section, clutching scraps of paper in their hands. Though nearly all the chairs in the hall were empty, no one used them. A few men who bore a slight resemblance to Karunakaran and mimicked his attitude were keeping an eye on the visitors. I approached one of them and told him who I was and the purpose of my visit. 'Wait here for ten minutes,' he said as he glanced at the files in my hand before walking away.

Heedless of the headmaster's warning, I drew up an empty chair and sat down. One of the men keeping watch over us was shocked at my insolence. He came over and stationed himself close to me. The middle-aged woman who stood behind me carrying a child in her arms looked at me with amazement. The child's legs were thin and shrunken. Drool was dribbling from its mouth. I wanted to chat with her. Deliberately raising my voice, I said, 'What happened to the child?' The woman, who had rotten teeth, remained silent as though she had not heard me. I asked her the same question again in an even louder voice. Looking alarmed, she turned to one of the men who were watching us. 'Is it the effect of polio?' I addressed my question directly to him.

'No, this is something else. The child is five years old but she says it still can't talk or walk. She has come to see the leader for his help in getting the child treated,' he explained; then asked, 'Are you from the school?' I thought he was trying to tell me that my behaviour was out of line. Then he started talking to a young man standing near the wall. Pretending to check the files I had brought with me, I lowered my head. To the sweaty old man who came up to me and inquired in a pitiful voice, 'Is the leader here?', I had no answer to give.

Karunakaran had emerged from inside the house just then, his bare chest covered by a thick mat of hair. Amid those bodies bent abjectly in anticipation of his mercy, I scrambled to my feet. In my nervousness, I let a file slip from my hand. Karunakaran watched me with an amused laugh as I ran hither and thither to retrieve the loose sheets that the wind was about to blow away.

~

LATER, I LOITERED AIMLESSLY FOR three days like an unhinged person. I had taken a day's leave on the false pretext of having to accompany Amma to the hospital. Since Sharada had planned to come to see Amma on Sunday, I avoided staying at home and went to the district capital to meet an old friend. When I returned after drinking with my friend untill late into the night, Sharada opened the door. I wanted her to be appalled by the smell of alcohol wafting from me. Pretending to be unsteady on my feet from intoxication, I went off to bed. In the morning, I lay feigning sleep until Sharada and her husband had left. When I was in office the next day, there was a call from

Sharada. 'What happened?' she asked. I replied as though I did not understand what she was talking about. 'Did you see him?' 'No,' I said. She must have been upset when I disconnected the call with evident irritation.

I opened the files on my desk, which had been left untouched for three days, and started answering the letters received from our district headquarters. A senior arts teacher who had applied for a loan from his provident fund account invited me to have tea with him. I walked with him to the tea stall, wondering all the way if I should tell him about Karunakaran. I thought obsessively about ways to bring Karunakaran's esteem down in the community. After recess, I sat alone in my sweltering office and wondered whether I should threaten him by sending an anonymous letter. Almost immediately, I abandoned the idea as juvenile and foolish. But it grew in my brain on its own, like a malignant tumour, or like a project, swiftly and secretly. I floundered, unable to control my still vengeful mind which kept formulating the required sentences and stashing them away. Rummaging through the files, I found Karunakaran's residential address and noted it down on a piece of paper. I decided that it would be safe to post the letter from the district capital which was quite far away. I sat in front of the typewriter with the air of someone typing official letters and promptly lost myself in rumination. As soon as I typed the first line, I realized that the letter could not be brief. Terrified by the steady traffic of teachers and colleagues through my office, the words began to hide and take cover.

I told the headmaster that I had to clear pending files and got his permission to spend the night in the office. The night watchman—who made his rounds with an air of sobriety while being moderately drunk—kept chatting with me all the while. He had an urgent wish to share with me all the secret, intoxicating stories he had collected about teachers and students. I listened to his stories as I waited impatiently for the moment when he would pass out. He asked me for money to buy a bottle of beer. I gave him three times the amount. He went to the market happily and came back with packets of food, a half-bottle of whisky and two beers. I lied that I was suffering from an upset stomach and refused to touch any of the items. Unable to stay up after dinner, the night watchman collapsed in a heap.

I sat uneasily on a wooden stool that had stiffened in the heat of the still ferocious late summer and started to type a threatening letter addressed to Karunakaran. Once begun, the letter galloped to a finish in no time, but since it was full of jagged sentences, it left me dissatisfied. I remained quiet for a long time, racking my brain for words that would give him the fright of his life. Then, having made up my mind, I described in full the cruel events of that nightmarish day in the form of a story that would remind him of those events even if he had forgotten them. The first part of the letter recounted how our lives had been ruined irrevocably; the second was about the vow of revenge I had made on that day and the intensity of my thirst for vengeance. Then, still mulling over the idea of fixing a deadline for killing him, I went to the school's playground and lit a cigarette.

I wanted the day of his murder to be a special day. I kept thinking, absurdly and theatrically, that it should happen on Karunakaran's or Sharada's birthday, or during the school's Annual Day or Independence Day celebrations. Just then, I heard the pulsating thumps of udukkais—double-sided, hourglass-shaped hand drums—coming from somewhere not far away. Having grown up in the shadow of itinerant storytellers like Kunnadaiya Kavundan, I had no difficulty in recognizing the subject of the intense recital. Most likely, it was the battlefield scene. The voice sounded as though it belonged to Kallamadai Ramasami Pandaram. It could have been Valanthankottai Chellappa Pandithan's too. Thrilled at having made a chance discovery, I walked in the direction of that sound with starlight for company. I stopped one of the men passing by on the foot trail and asked him about the performance. 'Yes, it is Valanthankottai Nasuvan (the barber from Valanthankottai) who is reciting the stories. It's been going on for twelve days now. Today it's the story of Nallathangal's lament. Everyone in the audience is crying and weeping. I couldn't bear it myself. What a horrible fate! It's only a story, I know, but who can bear this sorrow?'

I forged ahead with newfound vigour. A short distance away, Nallathangal was wailing in extreme anguish. As Nallathangal, with his thin ribcage covered by a short length of sari, Chellappa Pandithan swung his stilt-like legs and pranced around. Holding the udukkai close to his chest, he had plucked the unendurable torment of loss from the instrument and passed it on to the audience. The song lyrics that floated through the moist air, drenched with the tears of the audience, reminded me of Veerapur's dense forest filled with wunja trees, its blood-encrusted fields, the dilapidated Periya Kandiyamman temple, and the Koovandam Valley where water flowed in abundance. It was at that moment that I began to indulge in glorious fantasies of vengeance. Walking past the crowd, I came to a cluster of trees. As I stood in a small umbra of darkness and watched the performance, I was able to visualize the time and place for my act of revenge.

To take a short break and chew a round of betel, the singer handed the udukkai to an assistant and headed towards the pandal behind the temple. Accepting the invitation in his swollen, bleary eyes, I followed him.

'Is your mother better?'

'Can't say she is, Mama,' I said with a sigh.

'Did you take her to a hospital and have her looked at?'

'We do take her to the hospital now and then.'

The singer looked intently at me with his cold eyes as he chewed the betel wrap. 'Are the girls doing well?'

he asked. I didn't feel like replying. I was searching for Nallathangal's vengeful eyes in the singer's red-painted face.

'So, you heard me singing and came over, did you?'

'Yes, Mama. I was in the school to finish some pending work. When I heard your voice, I got up and came here.'

'How can anyone listen to this song and continue to work? Is it for nothing that so many people lie around in this dirt until daybreak?' He smiled, brimming with pride. Spitting out the betel juice, he stood up, removed and flapped his veshti, then wrapped it around his waist again. The udukkai was back in his hand.

'Stay back and watch the show untill the end.'

I gave him the slip and made my way back to the school.

In my mind, I thanked the singer for helping me transform a juvenile, anonymous letter into something with an epic quality. I came back to my office and, deciding on a date for taking revenge on Karunakaran, started to complete the letter. The clacking sounds from the collision of the typewriter's metal tongues with its roller lent an uneasy edge to the peaceful night. When I read through the letter, I thought it had turned out more perfect than I could have expected. Proud of myself for having taken a concrete first step in my plan for revenge, I read the letter again and again. Then, lighting a cigarette, I considered various strategies for posting it.

When I typed Karunakaran's address on the envelope, I used words that were neither neat nor accurate. I typed 'Panchayat Chairman' instead of the proper title, 'President, Town Panchayat', and 'Karunagaran Avargal' instead of 'Karunakaran'. I left the sender's address blank. I decided that I should post the letter only from the district capital and that I must not be on leave the next day. It was important to confuse him and not give him the faintest clue. I locked the office and pushed the key under the night watchman's pillow, then I wheeled my M-80 silently out of the compound.

On reaching the highway, I stopped at a deserted spot and kicked the starter pedal. Damp in the dewy air of dawn, the pathetic vehicle groaned like a chronically ill patient at first. Then, submitting to my brute force, it came to life with an alarming racket. In order to evade the prying eyes of that small town, I picked a shortcut and continued along that route. Once I had crossed twenty kilometres, I stopped at a roadside tea stall as its first customer of the day. Ordering a cup of tea, I started thinking about the sentences in the letter as I skimmed through the tattered pages of the previous day's *Dina Thanthi*. The stall owner's suspicious glance that settled on my profusely perspiring body made me uneasy. Mindful that I should leave before he started a conversation, I controlled my urge to smoke a cigarette. After a ten-minute ride, I stopped the vehicle at a lamp post by a bridge and, as I smoked, I took the letter out from the envelope and read the carefully typed sentences again.

After that, my M-80 didn't stop anywhere. As the streetlights began to go out one by one, I entered the district capital. I reckoned that it would be at least another two hours before the post office opened its doors. Looking for a place where I could wait until then, I reached the bus station just as it started to stir into action. Buying a newspaper, I sat down on a vacant cement bench in the waiting hall for passengers. I opened the letter inside the outspread pages of the newspaper and checked whether it contained any clue to the identity of the writer. I also wondered whether I had any reason for posting the letter in this distant town which had nothing to do with its contents. Trying to free myself from the torment of indecision, I smoked constantly. Then, propelled mainly by instinct, I left. Getting a refill of petrol from a station on the outskirts, I rode my moped on the empty highway at breakneck speed. At the end of an hour's journey, I was shocked to see where the M-80 had brought me. I trembled as I realized that there couldn't have been a more suitable post office for this letter.

Overwhelmed by the heat of the blood that rushed through all the veins and capillaries in my body, I gasped at the sight of the ramshackle building that seemed beyond redemption even now. The elderly head of the post office, visible behind the rusted iron grille of the counter, resembled the inconsolable ghost of my father who was once forcibly evicted from the same building. He didn't seem to mind that my hands trembled and tongue faltered when I bought a few stamps from him. He kept scrutinizing the ten-rupee note I had given him, trying to ascertain whether it was genuine.

'I have no change,' he said. He opened his desk drawer and pretended to check whether what he had just told me was indeed true, then he stuck out his lower lip. I resolved the problem swiftly by asking him to issue stamps for the whole amount. He grimaced as though my demand seemed outlandish to him. Then, since he had no other option, he counted the stamps slowly and pushed them into my hands. 'The glue is on the window sill,' he said, pointing in that direction. From a broken glass tumbler, I dug out a bit of the honey-brown neem resin that still had some moisture in it and spread it on the back of the stamps. Sitting at a very old wooden desk with wobbly legs, I pasted the stamps on the envelope and pushed it into a faded mailbox which must once have been bright red. Then I came out of the ancient-looking building which, from that moment on, had taken on a new importance for me. As I was stepping out, I glanced at Karunakaran's abandoned loan shop on the first floor, which looked the same as it had done thirty years ago. Without any logical reason, I sensed that I might have to come here again soon and the same incidents that had happened in the past could now occur again.

Determined to take me to the office before the designated time, my M-80 raced at a speed higher than it could normally achieve. I was on a protracted journey that could lead me to the most decisive moment of my life. Feeling the pleasure of having successfully completed the first step of that journey and the anxiety that came with imagining its subsequent stages, I sat idly on its seat. After half an hour, the loyal steed turned left at a canal that crossed my path near the foothills where I used to spend time as a child, travelled along a long dirt track that lay inert like a well-fed viper under the thick shade of babul trees, and stopped at a deserted spot. By then, its body was boiling hot. After instructing the vehicle to relax for some time, I looked for cover behind some bushes to perform my morning ablutions. Breaking off a twig from a neem tree, I cleaned my teeth with it. Then I took off my clothes and stepped into the cool water of the canal. An Indian ratsnake lying on the dense nutgrass shrubs on the bank took fright, sprang into the canal and swam past me to disappear into a vortex.

I came across a barber in a village on the way, and got a shave and combed my hair. Then I rode the vehicle carefully towards my office. It passed the school gates well before the first bell. Startled at first on hearing the tremendous racket it made, the children laughed in ridicule and ran off. Paying them no heed, I went to my office and instructed the assistant who had just entered to bring me the files

I needed. 'Do you have to send any particulars urgently, Sir?' The assistant was only trying to ease my anxiety with his flippant question. In no mood to respond, I began to sort the files into different stacks.

I checked whether the teachers' applications for medical leave had been submitted as per the prescribed procedure. I summoned the teachers who had neither maintained the students' attendance registers properly nor filled in the required details, and instructed them to update the registers within the next two days. I was aware that my activities as a mere clerk who had no direct authority surprised and annoyed the headmaster. I lied to him that a friend of mine who worked in the district office had told me the district education officer might turn up unannounced for an inspection. The headmaster looked somewhat apprehensive. Taking advantage of the situation, I drafted a harshly worded circular, got the headmaster's approval and sent it to all the teachers in the school. I too worked hard, filling in the missing details in the work registers I was responsible for, keeping my own register up to date and compiling educational statistics. The teachers were rushing about here and there with the attendance registers for their respective classes. The headmaster, who was still incredulous about the power of his authority, made regular rounds of the campus, keeping an eye on everyone. Seeing the cane swinging in his hand, the students took fright and tried to take cover. When I noticed the teachers trying to smile every time they ran into me, I was intoxicated by my own phantom authority.

I buried myself in the files even as I wondered how I was going to face Karunakaran when he came to the school after receiving the letter tomorrow or the day after. I spent those two days trying to create a trustworthy and respectable image of myself before the headmaster and other teachers. To quell the anxiety that was prowling like a nocturnal animal through my veins, I started chatting affably with the teachers during recess. I bantered endlessly and humorously about jokes that had appeared in films and weekly magazines, and about disappointments over the recent Pay Commission report. In the afternoon, I assisted some teachers with their attendance registers. I also grew tired fairly soon.

At home, an impatient Sharada was waiting for me. She had brought her son along for company but, unable to withstand his nagging, she was already preparing to leave. She told me that she had come early that morning and wanted to know where I had been all night. Ignoring the lies I told her, she stared with suspicion at my dirty clothes and bleary eyes. When I went to the bedroom to see Amma, she followed me. Amma's condition appeared to have improved a little. As soon as she saw me, Amma started complaining about my younger sister and burst into tears. She asked me the same questions that Sharada had. Without replying, I went inside to change my clothes.

I wondered whether I should tell Sharada about the letter. I had guessed that she would stay back at home to find out what I had been up to. I had even kept a copy of the typed letter in my briefcase to show her. Just as I was taking it out of the envelope, my younger sister appeared with a cup of coffee. After that, we had no opportunity to talk in private until Sharada said goodbye and left. Before leaving, she whispered, 'Whatever you may want to do, don't do it without telling me.'

To escape the noise from the television, I placed a string cot under the tamarind tree in front of my house and lay down. I felt that the heat was turning my body into vapour. Karunakaran would be upset on receiving the letter, I thought, and he would try to recall my face and that distant day from the recesses of his memory. I wanted him to feel on his dead tongue the salt of the tears that had flowed from Sharada's brown eyes as she stood before him trembling like a wounded bird. He would never have imagined that I would follow him like a vengeful serpent and that he would struggle to protect himself from the panic that would follow. I smiled to myself. I also wished fervently that he should somehow discover my identity.

The next day, I was dressed a bit more elegantly than usual when I set out for office. I had washed my dusty moped and wiped it clean. I reached the office feeling brave and confident. To protect the image that I had built, I set about my tasks at a brisk pace. I felt that being a person of importance who was noticed by everyone, or acting like one at any rate, would keep me safe. I believed that it would come to my aid when that critical moment arrived, though there was no logical basis for thinking so. Just as I had expected, Karunakaran did not come to work that day. I thought the letter might not have been delivered yet. Both relieved and disappointed at the postponement of that decisive moment I had been waiting for, I returned home. I slept fitfully in the company of nightmares replete with daredevil feats, and woke up at dawn.

I couldn't avoid meeting Karunakaran the next day, or so I thought. But he did not turn up the next two days as well. His ash-grey car which I used to see every day on the national highway that passed by the town was missing. I suspected that the letter might not have reached him. Or perhaps he had chosen to ignore it. Frightened by the gravity of the charges in the letter, he could be lying low at home. I also wondered whether he might have fled town.

I could put all my doubts to rest very quickly through a simple ruse. I lied to the headmaster that in the copy of a resolution of the PTA we had to get a few signatures from Karunakaran, who was in charge as its president, and send it to the district office. I requested the headmaster to send an assistant to Karunakaran's house for the purpose. The headmaster told me that he was not in town and would be away for a couple of days.

The next two days were unbearable. Unable to shield myself from the heat of vengeance blazing within me, I spent the nights driving my old M-80 around aimlessly. At about an hour past midnight, I went to see Sharada at her home. Except her, everyone in the house was asleep. When she opened the door, my eyes fell instantly on the television set which was on at a low volume. She was excited by my untimely visit. She thought that something must have happened. Careful not to wake those who were asleep, she greeted me in a low whisper. 'What brings you here at this late hour?' she asked nervously at first; then she recovered quickly and said, 'Amma is all right, isn't she?' Roused from his sleep by the faint sounds occasioned by my visit, her husband ascertained that I hadn't brought any worrisome news and went back to the bedroom. 'Are you hungry?' she asked. Unable to read a response in my tired eyes, she went to the kitchen. I followed her. She took a bowl each of sambar and rasam from the refrigerator and heated them. While I ate, she sat before me and gave me a pitiful look.

I sighed. I wanted to be kind to her and tell her something about what was going on, and so I described very briefly all that I had done. When I told her about the letter, she looked deeply troubled. Without a word, she got up and left. I put my plate in the sink, washed my hands and came to the hall. She had spread a mat on the floor for me. 'No, I'll be off now,' I said and prepared to set out immediately.

'Why are you leaving now, at this unearthly hour? Stay back and go in the morning,' she said. I stopped her from coming to the door to see me off and stepped out. Feeling helpless and angry that I could not make her understand my plan and its immediate fallout, I kick-started my vehicle. Mercilessly ruining the sleep of people who had buried their tired bodies in the cold solitude of the hours past midnight, I rode my noisy moped home. Ignoring Amma, who whimpered attempting to say something as soon as she saw me, I went straight to bed. I kept brooding for a long time about what awaited me on the morrow.

The next day, too, I reached the office half an hour early. Karunakaran's ash-grey car was parked under the red laburnum tree that stood like a giant umbrella in front of the office. This was completely unexpected. I was taken aback. My vengeful heart started pounding. The black smoke streaming angrily from the exhaust pipe of my vehicle enveloped me as if trying to protect me. Determined to be defiant and brave while facing him, I entered my office room. Karunakaran was sitting restively in the headmaster's chair. The headmaster was scouring the special cupboard where confidential and important files were kept. Karunakaran looked at me as soon as I entered. I greeted him and went to my seat on the other side of the wooden partition. When I saw the files strewn haphazardly on my desk, I guessed that someone else must have taken them down from the shelf. I began to sense the arrival of anxiety's heavy footsteps in my heart. My body began to tremble from the humiliation of having been caught out so easily. I concluded that the letter must have contained an obvious clue and I tried to put the files in order as I brooded over it. Then I summoned the office assistant and asked him what had happened. He whispered into my ear that the assistant headmaster and the physical education teacher had opened my cupboard and brought out all the important files, searching for something in them. Since I didn't quite know how to respond, I kept quiet. It was then that Karunakaran called for me.

'Is the clerk here? Tell him that I want to see him. Clerk Sir, will you step in here for a minute, please?' he called out in a loud voice. I had no option but to face him. I went and stood before him, calm and steady. Unable to sit comfortably on the wire-mesh seat of the headmaster's chair, Karunakaran seemed ill at ease. His wandering eyes, moving like marbles behind his spectacles, indicated that he didn't consider me a creature worthy of his attention. Removing his glasses and wiping them slowly and carefully, he looked intently at me with his dim, ash-grey eyes. As if trying to enunciate a decisive phrase, his lips were forming a pout. In the chess game that had commenced between us, it seemed he was thinking hard about his first move. I reminded myself that it was my duty as an honest player to give him enough time and opportunity to think.

'Your name?' I told him. Then he asked me where I was staying and about my family. Mindful that I must not lie, I answered his questions. He remained silent for some time. When the headmaster finally finished rummaging through the cupboard, he had a tattered brown file in his hands. Opening it with reverence, he scrutinized it carefully for a few minutes until his eyes lit up. I could tell at once that he had found whatever he had been searching for all this while. Then he stood to Karunakaran's left, contorting his body in an awkward fashion to avoid any physical contact with his shoulder, held the file open at an angle that made it clearly visible to Karunakaran, and started explaining something to him in a subdued and abject tone. I wondered insolently whether I should sit in one of the empty chairs in front of him. Sensing my impatience, Karunakaran turned towards me abruptly.

'Clerk Sir, will you come by my house this evening?' he said, looking directly into my eyes. Since it did not seem like an order, I didn't know how to respond and kept quiet. 'I need you to look over my accounts for a bit. My accountant has been ill. It's been two months since he last came to my house. It would help if you could come by,' he added in a cold, unemotional voice.

The beast of my vengeance began to roll its tongue in greedy anticipation. Without betraying any emotion, I indicated my consent and returned to my seat. Just when I began to realize that at the commencement of this strange game, he and I were standing obediently before a destiny common to both of us, the telephone rang. For some reason, I thought the caller must be Sharada. I wanted him to be the one to pick up the receiver on the headmaster's table. Thinking about the opportunity that had come Sharada's way after so many years and imagining its consequences excited me. Meanwhile, he picked up the receiver and held it against his right ear.

'Vanakkam. Please tell me.' I thought that despite the thirty years which had gone by so quickly, Sharada would have recognized his voice. 'He is here. Who shall I say is calling?'

I pricked up my ears to find out if she would tell him her name. But he dropped his voice even lower. I stood up and walked towards the headmaster's table as if I was looking for a rubber stamp. On seeing me, Karunakaran, who was listening with a blank expression on his face, said, 'He is here. Hold on, I'll put him on.' He was about to remove the receiver from his ear when I stood before him. If he had not said, 'Paramanandam Sir, call for you,' as he held out the receiver towards the assistant headmaster who had just poked his head into the room, my foolishness or agitation would have been exposed. With a sense of relief, I picked up a rubber stamp that I had no use for from the headmaster's table and returned to my seat.

At dusk, as signs of impending rain began to appear, I stood in front of his house like a lowly servant. Since the man was in his farmhouse, I was instructed to wait in the veranda. A middle-aged woman with uneven teeth and a decrepit body, and a young woman who was her exact opposite in appearance, were watching me intently from the veranda. The young woman's face, visible through hexagonal gaps in the bamboo screen that separated the veranda from the front yard, was extraordinarily beautiful—like Sharada's when she had been ravaged by Karunakaran's ruthless hands thirty years ago. I presumed nervously that she could not be his daughter. However, it was my misfortune to learn within the next few minutes that she was indeed his offspring. She got up as soon as she saw me and, holding the hem of her long skirt up above her ankles to avoid tripping, stepped down from the veranda and came towards me. Mentally drawing a line four feet away from me, she examined me with eyes that were as wide as paddles, swimming in an ocean of innocence. She asked me in a commanding tone who I was and why I was waiting there. I felt powerless to respond to her and my eyes lacked the courage to face her beauty. I remained silent. As if taken aback by her somewhat sharp tone when she repeated the question, I told her in a subdued voice the purpose of my visit. Then she told me that her father was on the farm and would meet me in five minutes. She went back into the house and disappeared.

Before leaving, she said, 'Please sit down there,' pointing to the row of blue plastic chairs in the veranda.

Under a pandal covered by vines of royal jasmine, its flowers, which were the colour of light, lay scattered. I picked one up. A middle-aged woman handed me a cup of coffee. She could be his wife, I thought.

But in the next one hour I spent in that house, I learnt that his wife was indeed the woman with the wrecked body and uneven teeth. He had a son too. The son seemed to have inherited the uneven teeth and unhealthy body from his mother, and the lust-filled eyes, wide nostrils and stocky build from his father. The daughter seemed to have taken after someone totally unrelated to both. I think she was the prime reason for my becoming an intimate member of that family within the next fortnight.

When he emerged from the farm, Karunakaran apologized profusely for making me wait. After checking whether I had been offered coffee, he led me past the finely appointed veranda to his office room. He pointed me to a comfortable chair that lay buried under a jumble of files and ledgers. He was the proprietor of two or three finance companies and a stone quarry. He was also a partner in a local movie theatre and a spinning mill. I learnt that his wife and daughter were contractors for many public works of the local municipality. The stone quarry functioned under his direct oversight and he visited it every day without fail. He had built a small site office there. The office for coordinating all these businesses was situated in a section of his house. It functioned under his daughter's supervision.

He called her Sulo. Must be short for Sulochana, I thought. I issued a stern warning to my heart, covered by frozen slabs of love that had begun to melt once I laid eyes on her, not to fall in love with her. Otherwise this tale of revenge might turn into one of those inane love stories in third-rate Tamil films.

Barring his elderly accountant who was in poor health, the employees in his office were idiots. From a young man with a slender physique, who looked like he could recite the numbers from one to hundred without pausing for breath, I received the ledgers and bill books under my charge. From then on, with the headmaster's blessings, I left the office at around four in the afternoon every day and arrived at Karunakaran's house. A cup of coffee, along with biscuits, would be waiting for me. With the assistance of the young man who could recite from one to hundred, I would begin the challenging task of putting the chaotic accounts in order. First his son, and then Sulo, would return from college. The son—I learnt his name was Gowthaman—would come directly to the office room. Eyes alert and watchful, he would lounge for some time in his father's chair. He would touch a few of the ledgers I had spread on the desk—cautiously, as if handling an insect. He would then turn the pages with even deeper circumspection. With his immobile eyes, he would keep staring vacantly at the numbers that were perched like flies inside the dark blue squares. When, in a secret ambush, confusion began to cleave his plump, smooth-as-clay face in two, he would close the ledger and get up from the chair. Then he would call someone from his father's telephone. Wedging the receiver between his ear and shoulder, he would roll a paperweight idly between his fingers as he talked. During the conversation, he would often laugh out loud or scream in anger. Sometimes he would talk in a subdued tone that no human ear could discern. The thick gold chain around his neck, the bracelet on his wrist and the vulgar rings on each finger seemed to testify that he was a useless creature. A small milk-white car and a motorcycle were available exclusively for his use. When I saw those perfectly noiseless vehicles, I guessed that his shadowy world outside the house must be one that turned on the axis of crime.

Occasionally, Sulo would come to the office room. She would ask me questions that were eminently forgettable. As though she realized only after coming into the room that the string of flowers in her hair had wilted, she would extricate it from her thick braid and fling it into the dustbin on top of the crumpled balls of paper that I had thrown in there.

Sulo liked to thread pink-edged royal jasmine flowers into a string and wear it in her hair. On some days, she favoured new varieties of roses that had yellow, pale red and violet petals, long stems and one or two leaves. She must have bought those no-longer-fresh flowers from a woman vendor by the roadside on her way back from college. After carefully picking and removing those still-radiant flowers from her hair, she would hold them in her palms for some time and then let them slide very gently, liquid like, into the dustbin. Whenever I sat alone in that room after she left, the fragrance that rose from the carcasses of those flowers would remind me of her. To collect myself, I would bury my nose in the ledgers and begin to inhale the musty smell of paper.

I confessed everything to Sharada. She gave me a severe scolding. She accused me of drowning myself in foolish fantasies. I was taken aback. When she had simmered down and started breathing normally, I explained the finer details of my plan to her. Growing impatient, she interrupted my account.

'All right. What are you going to *do*?'

I told her I didn't understand.

'How are you going to kill him?' Crinkling her brown eyes, she looked directly at me. I was stumped by the question.

'Some day, after I've earned his complete trust, I can mix poison in his coffee or food.'

She burst into laughter. I felt humiliated, as if I had suddenly become a caricature. She berated me harshly for not having freed myself yet from the naivety and fantasies of that ridiculous little boy who had stood with a raised sickle in his hand thirty years ago. She had visualized other ways of killing him. It must be an unforgettable and horrible sight, she said. I realized that she wanted to see, with her own vengeful eyes, Karunakaran lying on the ground, his body split open with a deadly weapon. Unable to give her hope with my timorous voice, I fumbled.

Then she advised me to be extremely careful. All said, she couldn't stop herself from appreciating the opportunity we now had to get close to him. She told me that from my vantage point inside the house, I should keep a close watch on his movements and identify a time and circumstance that would allow him no chance of escape. She also asked me about the letter. She worried that he might not have received it, that I had perhaps failed to write the address properly. Promising her that I would try to confirm his receipt of the letter and think of a new strategy, I left with a feeling of unease.

When I met Karunakaran the next time, I tried to infer from his body language if he had received my letter. When no one was around, I opened his desk drawer and checked for the envelope I had sent. I scoured the piles of invitations and greeting cards that lay unopened on the window sills and in the cupboards. I was bewildered by his increasing reliance on me. Perhaps it was because I had straightened out many irregularities in his accounts and transactions in the past two weeks, I reasoned. As Sharada said, he might not have bothered about the letter. I felt ashamed to have imagined that I could threaten a man who was hidden safely inside a fortress of power with an anonymous letter.

I continued to mull over potentially effective and practical ways to achieve our goal.

I had become a person of importance for his wife and other members of the household. I was a big help to them when it came to fulfilling small needs. I managed to procure through a friend in Chennai a physics textbook that Sulo needed within a week. When I heard that his son was injured on the forehead while playing cricket with his friends, I picked him up immediately and rushed to the hospital. Because of these minor acts of heroism, Sulochana became more friendly towards me. She was impressed by the books I brought with me to read. She had begun to hold long, childlike conversations with me on films and political developments. I became one of the few people who could lounge comfortably in the veranda of their house.

After auditing the income and expenditure accounts of Karunakaran's quarry, I discovered irregularities committed by the person in charge and alerted Karunakaran that fraud to the tune of several lakhs of rupees had taken place. From that day, the doors of that house were kept open for me. When I was formally invited to have lunch with Karunakaran, the headmaster looked at me in awe. I had begun to receive extra respect from the teachers. Barring a few complicated tasks, the headmaster became used to getting the rest of my work done with the help of the drawing teacher who barely had any classes to teach.

By now, the profits from Karunakaran's businesses had doubled. Everything he touched seemed to sparkle. I even wondered whether this man, who was gaining steadily in maturity, was at all a suitable target for revenge. His successes made me extremely jealous. The cruel arms of his mercy that stretched out to offer me benediction were destroying my peace of mind.

This was a phase in my life when misfortune had begun to engulf me. Amma's health was deteriorating with each passing day. There was much bitterness and rancour between my sisters over having to care for her. Sharada's husband met with an accident and was admitted to a hospital with multiple fractures in his thigh bones. My ancient M-80 had become completely decrepit. The ordeals I suffered every day trying to start the vehicle as I left my office had become a source of entertainment for the students. Karunakaran, who paid me meagre amounts every now and then as compensation for my services, came forward to help me replace my pathetic vehicle. I was firm in my refusal. The next day, his wife and Sulo insisted that I should accept his help.

I found it intolerable when Sulo began to tease me about my vehicle. Spending a sizeable amount from my salary for the month, I got the silencer cleaned, which reduced the noise. Then I changed the torn seat cover and got an oil service done, and the vehicle improved somewhat. That afternoon, when my M-80 arrived and stopped in front of their house without making any sound, Sulo was so amazed that she ran inside to call her mother.

I began to suspect that I had fallen in love with her. I worried that this might unavoidably turn into a preposterous love story, just as I had feared. Sharada, who had come to visit my mother, noted with alacrity the name 'Sulo' that came up frequently in our conversation. After much reflection, she told me that we had to visit a temple the coming Tuesday, and instructed me to keep my refurbished vehicle ready with a full tank of fuel. I was beginning to feel depressed, as though I was being assailed by some mysterious force. I requested the headmaster for a week's medical leave. All of Monday, I lay curled up at home. At five in the afternoon, there was a call from Karunakaran. I lied to him that I was running a fever.

'Since when?' he inquired with concern. Then he asked me whether I had seen a doctor and offered to send his family physician. I replied that I had already seen a doctor and it might take me two or three days to be fit enough to go to his house. The telephone rang again at eight that evening.

'How is your health?' I was astonished to hear Sulo's soft, gentle voice. I suspected that she was calling me secretly, unbeknownst to anyone in her house.

'Fever?'

'Yes.'

'Just normal fever, right?'

'Yes. The climate doesn't suit me.'

'Did you see a doctor?'

I told her the same lie I had told her father.

'Will you come tomorrow?'

'No, it might take two or three days.'

'Come for a casual visit, then. You don't have to do any work.'

Afraid that I might not be able to stop myself from falling apart, I disconnected the call.

That night, I came down with a fever for real. Without worrying about it, I slept as usual on the string cot under the tamarind tree. My younger sister, who had got up at midnight to go to the bathroom, heard me groaning, came over and discovered that I was burning up. She prepared hot water and gave me a few pills from my mother's stock. Though it seemed to subside slightly, the fever intensified as the night wore on. I began to babble in delirium. Frightened, my sister called Sharada on the telephone. At dawn, I was taken to a hospital in a taxi. When I returned home, carrying my tired body which vindicated my lie, Sulo was in the house. She was sitting on the filthy plastic chair in front of my mother's bed, letting the fragrance of royal jasmine waft through our dilapidated house. Sharada and I were shocked to see her.

Sulo said she had stopped by to see me on her way to college. To Sharada and to other unimportant characters in this story, such as my mother and younger sister, she introduced herself as my 'friend'. Amma must have regained consciousness just a short while before Sulo arrived, I thought. When Amma stroked her forehead with her withered fingers, Sulo was overcome by shyness and bit her lip. Handing over the oranges and apples that she had brought to my younger sister, she looked at me. 'When Appa told me that you were sick, I couldn't believe it. I thought you said it just to fool us. I brought all this fruit only as a formality. Looking at you now, I know the fever must have been terrible,' she said and got up to leave. Sharada, who was sitting on the edge of my mother's bed, kept staring at Sulo with her brown eyes. I noticed that greed was aflame in my younger sister's eyes. When Sulo started her scooty, my sister ran up to her as though she had just thought of it, shouting, 'Wait! Have a cup of coffee and go.' Sulo smiled. 'Only coffee? No meal on offer?' she said, laughing, and left after promising to visit again.

My eyesight began to grow dim. Worried that I might recover from the fever too quickly, I tried my best to look even more sickly. When my sister was not around, I chain-smoked cigarettes. After she went to sleep at night, I came out of the house and walked in the open to catch the falling dew. As expected, the fever worsened the next day. Sulo kept calling me at odd hours when no one would expect her to call. She said she would talk to her father and arrange to send a doctor. Just as I was declining her offer in a feeble voice, my sister snatched the receiver from me. Reciting a litany of complaints about me, she said, 'Why don't you tell him to straighten up?' Then she whined some more about my smoking. 'He doesn't listen to any of us. You could tell him, no?' she said and handed the receiver back to me.

'Are you a little boy, then? Won't you listen when people tell you?' Sulo scolded me, addressing me in the singular, without honorifics. I was startled. Quickly, she apologized. 'Sorry, 'pa.' Even her apology sounded intimate. Embarrassed, my sister moved away.

In the next half hour, Gowthaman's car arrived at our door. Gowthaman, who was accompanied by a doctor, mustered a semblance of kindness in his swollen eyes and inspected our poverty-stricken house. I watched helplessly as the driver handed over two big shopping bags full of fruit to my sister. When my sister, who was trapped irretrievably in the grip of their mercy, propped the two bags against the wall, one of them slid down, making the apples and oranges roll across the veranda. As the doctor pressed and examined my eyelids, I saw with my teary eyes that his own, which were brown like Sharada's, were boring into me.

Sharada had transformed into a ferocious beast. She no longer possessed the vocabulary to speak to me. With her son in tow, she wandered all over the area in search of temples whose deities were endowed with the power of retribution and offered heartfelt prayers for revenge. When I heard that she had gone to Masani Amman temple a week ago, ground a kilo of red chillies into powder and anointed the deity with the paste, I was astonished. I also heard that she had stood at the entrance of Mooduparai Karuppannan temple in a wet sari and impaled two chicks on the spears planted in the ground there. Her husband, however, laughed it off, saying that she indulged in such foolish acts only to punish some women in their neighbourhood who were giving her endless trouble. The blood drained from my face as I listened to him.

Two weeks later, she stood on my doorstep at dawn on a Tuesday morning. Her hair was open and wild like that of vengeful female deities. I could almost hear the blood pulsing through the swollen arteries that throbbed on her forehead, left bare like a widow's.

'Let's go,' she said.

'Where?'

'It's an emergency. Let's go.'

'What kind of emergency—and at this unearthly hour?' My sister, who had woken up and joined us, wanted to know.

'Start right now. I'll tell you later.' Sharada ordered me in a belligerent voice that demanded obedience. I stepped out without a word. My sister was stunned. When she asked in a flippant tone, 'Is anyone proposing a bride for Annan? Tell me. Let me also come along and see her,' there was no answer from Sharada.

My M-80 raced ahead, following its own route as usual. From thirty to twenty-nine, twenty-nine to twenty-eight, then twenty-seven … subtracting the years one by one, it led us towards the past, to the small town which was once our home. Along the highway, the jamun trees which we used to climb as children had reached maturity. The clusters of wunja trees in the fields adjoining the town's boundaries seemed to have increased. But like memorials of a past era, the town's moss-covered buildings and their broken compound walls were still in the same condition. Not even a single new branch had sprung from the portia trees. At the entrance of the Annanmar temple, which looked like a peasant's old tile-roofed house, the plaster horse mounts of the folk heroes Ponnar-Shankar standing with their front legs raised, tails aloft, and foaming at the mouth, had been given a fresh coat of paint. It was the only change we could see. Light reflecting from the broken glass pieces embedded in their cracked saddles dazzled the eye. The shepherd who was perched atop the temple's boundary wall on his haunches looked at us intently. The sheep which had been released minutes ago into the pastures on either side of the temple looked like they had been grazing there for thirty years.

As though we had no connection with anyone in that town, we crossed the deserted market ground and headed straight towards the post office. Sighing deeply, a diffident Sharada stepped on to the veranda. Time, which had lain frozen for thirty years, began to melt at the touch of her breath. The elderly postmaster across the counter looked up at us in surprise. I imagined that he was trying to place me. In order not to arouse suspicion, I decided to buy a few stamps.

'One inland letter.' He looked suspiciously at my right hand, which was extended past the window. Raising his wrinkled face, he said, 'But I don't have change!' and searched in the drawer of his table. 'No problem. Give me stamps for the balance amount,' I said. Wincing as though he was embarrassed, the postmaster counted the stamps carefully and pushed them into my hand. 'Everything that's happened before seems to recur again and again,' he said wearily. 'Yes,' I whimpered. Meanwhile, Sharada had begun to climb the stairs on the side of the building. Stuffing the inland letter and the stamps into my shirt pocket, I hurried after her. The steps were broken. Karunakaran's loan shop on the first floor was wide open, as though it had been abandoned. The door had been removed from the doorframe and propped up against the wall. In the veranda, which was strewn with garbage and filth, lay an empty beer bottle and scattered shards of broken glass. In one corner, a ragged blanket that someone had left behind lay in tatters. Seeing a troop of ants dragging a used condom that had been flung near the wall, Sharada recoiled in shock. Emboldened by my arrival, she stepped into the room. 'I was here,' she pointed to the spot and sighed. With her brown eyes that looked as though they were frozen by time, she was gazing at the walls where the plaster had fallen off in many places. As if she wanted to find a sentence of the curse that would destroy Karunakaran, she was searching for something on the floor.

I came out quietly. The spot where I had stood holding a sickle aloft in my callow hand, impelled by a thirst for revenge inappropriate for my age, was near this cement pillar that was still intact. Then I remembered how Karunakaran had walked over to me, reeking of sweat. The memory of how he had gripped the sickle in his rough, hairy hands and said, 'Do you watch a lot of movies, da?' as he snatched it from me with a laugh, came back to me. When I heard someone sobbing and looked up, Sharada was already halfway down the stairs. After collecting and securing the harsh, final sentence of the curse that Sharada had found there, I followed her. The whole town was watching our movements with close attention. The faces that passed us in the streets looked very familiar. I thought one of them might suddenly call both of us by name. Then I wanted to see the poky little house where we used to live. When I turned to Sharada, who was seated on the pillion, to tell her about my wish, she remained silent, as though she didn't want to respond. By then, my M-80 had travelled a long way past the town limits. I suspected that she was crying. To appease her and diffuse the tension, I ventured to ask her a different question—about her son's passion for cricket. Since she did not reply to this one either, I slowed down and turned to look at her face. The pillion seat was empty.

Every time we met, Sulo sent me coded signals. She had unfolded the soft, pink-edged petals of her love for me. With the aim of turning her into an instrument of my vengeance, I too sent her a few signals of my own. I decided to take the first step in this revenge saga through a kiss and waited for a moment's privacy. Though private moments were not rare, I let the opportunities slip on purpose. Feigning a complete lack of interest in her, I focused my entire attention, with scarcely a break, on completing the tasks that Karunakaran had assigned to me. Without being aware of it, I had turned into his shadow. Delegating the responsibility of managing his industries and businesses to me, Karunakaran had begun to concentrate on the fulfilment of his political ambitions. I had suddenly become worthy of the attention and respect of the residents of that town. Whenever I stood near the corner shop enjoying a smoke or simply loitered around without purpose, I noticed that complete strangers tried to smile at me or occasionally raised their hands to pay respects. It made me nervous. The headmaster had passed a few requests to Karunakaran through me and got them fulfilled; he was overjoyed. A teacher-colleague asked me for help with his transfer. I gave Karunakaran a photocopy of his application and he spoke to the education minister immediately on the telephone. When my colleague received his transfer order from the Directorate of School Education within a week, I was shocked. By helping a few of my relatives to obtain bank loans and title deeds for residential plots through Karunakaran's intervention, I had become respectable in their eyes.

I went to the school whenever I could find the time. Even when there was no pressure, I made a habit of staying in the office beyond midnight and completing my tasks at demonic speed. It was a time when luck had begun to descend on Karunakaran. Profit from his businesses had seen tremendous growth. The party with which he was affiliated had given him an important position at the district level. There were indications that in the Assembly elections slated for next year, he was going to contest from his area. The house was constantly besieged by party members. He was trying to get guidance and cooperation from many different types of men. He toured relentlessly, meeting and listening to people, learning about their grievances and finding solutions for them. He took me along on many occasions. We spent long hours in his farmhouse discussing political developments. An additional responsibility of providing him the information and statistics that he needed for speeches at public meetings and discussions with his party colleagues was also assigned to me. When he started introducing me in his political circles as his close friend, I felt I was caught in a trap. He purchased a new motorcycle for my use. I declined it, and continued to ride my M-80. Sulo tried to intervene in the matter.

'Ei, what's wrong, 'pa? It seems you won't use the bike we bought for you?' she came to the office that evening and complained.

'No. Why do I need all that? This M-80 will do for someone in my position,' I said.

'So you are talking about status and all? If you want to hold yourself apart from us, don't come here any more, understand?' After stomping out in high dudgeon, she rushed back almost immediately. Her eyes were red. I thought she might have cried. 'So when you mix with us, we are strangers to you, are we?' she asked me with childish pathos, sitting down in front of me. With her delicate fingers she stroked my hand resting idly on the table. 'Please try to understand,' she said apropos of nothing.

In person and on the telephone, Sulo was given to pleading constantly for love. She introduced me to her friends. For silly reasons, she would take me along on outings to the city. Returning early from college and ordering me to leave the school and come right away, she seemed desperate. I obliged her even as I nurtured a secret plan in my mind of using her love to wreak vengeance on Karunakaran.

Gowthaman had begun to host parties every night in a cottage built especially for him on the compound. His circle of friends seemed highly suspect to me. Whenever he came by the office, he reeked of alcohol. Since he was bunking college and making merry with his friends the entire time, he had begun to pester me for money from the office account far in excess of his needs. At one point, when I brought this to Karunakaran's attention, he refused to bother about it. 'Leave it,' he said, dismissing the matter in two words.

Bereft of any connection with her son, husband or anyone else, Sulo's mother lounged all day in a specially designed cane armchair in the veranda of that huge mansion, as though she was eternally waiting for some mysterious person. The pallor of disease was spreading fast through her body. Oblivious to the rancid smell that wafted from her breath, she wallowed in her pride about her husband's good fortune. For some reason, I was hesitant to take the first step in my journey of revenge. With Sulo, who sought the warmth of love amid the scalding heat of my vengeful heart, I was very careful. I had not said a word to her about the sorrows that had begun to engulf me.

Even so, Sulo inquired with concern whenever we happened to meet every day.

'How is Amma?'

'Not bad. She is getting on.'

'Is she eating properly?'

'Hmm … of course, yes.'

'Does she think of me? I know she doesn't, because you must not have told her about me.'

But death's milk-white teeth had begun to gnaw at Amma's life. I was firm in my resolve that I must not share my troubles with Sulo or anyone else in that family. Every time she came to visit Amma, Sharada went back with tears in her eyes. Whenever she learnt about the good fortune that seemed to follow Karunakaran, dark circles of disappointment would begin to spread around her eyes. As cranes did with their nests, she had learned to hide her sorrows in places no one could discover. In a low, soft whisper that was audible only to me, she would curse Karunakaran and the gods who generously bestowed the bounties of destiny on him. 'It's true what they say, that god gives to evil folks everything they ask for,' she would whimper in a voice enveloped by the fog of helplessness and take her leave.

Her curses lacked the power to affect Karunakaran.

Sulo was receiving alliance proposals from some of the wealthiest families. In a household teeming with marriage brokers and astrologers, I was becoming a person unworthy of anyone's attention. Work that was making me gasp, giving me no time for regular meals, had wrung my neck and cast me among the ledgers. Before every man who came to meet her formally, Sulo stood demurely as a prospective bride, overcome with shyness, draped in expensive zari-embroidered silk saris. During these occasions, I didn't step out of the office room. After they had left, she would come looking for me. She would fill my tabletop with sweets and snacks made for the guests and insist that I sample them. She would go on about the special traits of the prospective groom who had come to meet her that day. Knowing that she wanted to make me jealous, I pretended that I had no interest in such matters. In truth, I found the situation unbearable. Whenever the alliance didn't work out for some reason, I derived a mean pleasure out of it. When I learnt that she had not rejected anyone and that finalizing a groom was getting postponed only because of extraneous reasons such as the matching of horoscopes or family backgrounds, I began to torment myself with jealousy. Finally, she told me herself that with all the horoscope matches in place, the son of an oil-mill owner had been selected as her groom. Standing in front of me, with her silk sari rustling as she fidgeted, she asked with a wink, 'Do you know that they are going to get me married?' Keeping my face impassive as a rock, I nodded.

'Don't you feel bad?'

'Why should I feel bad about it?'

'You wretch! Don't you love me, then?'

I said 'No' without a hint of mercy and looked intently at her face. Her face had turned red. Her eyes were filled with tears. Sighing, I lowered my gaze back to the files. She got up suddenly. Unnerved, I rose quickly from my chair. Her body stiff, she approached me and pulled me towards her like prey, then gave me a kiss that I would never forget in my lifetime. Before I could feel its taste, she released me and ran out of the room.

Staring with dread at the strand of her hair that stretched like a worm across my fingernails, I stood paralysed in a stranger's home, in the office of a man on whom I was waiting to wreak vengeance. My lips were aflame. Time was crumbling to ash. I couldn't tell whether it was in the past or the present that I was standing atop this heap of time's ashes. I also tried to pretend that this had happened to someone else. My frail body began to warm up like a parched riverbed. As the portent of some misfortune, the office telephone began to ring.

My hands trembled. As expected, it was a call from my sister. Without giving me a specific reason, she asked me to come home right away. Though I didn't hear another word of her anxious voice, I knew for certain that Amma had passed away. I left immediately without informing anyone. At home, apart from Amma's lifeless body and my sister who had faced Amma's death all by herself, a few women from the neighbouring houses were present, announcing the death through their wails and cries.

I entered the veranda where Amma's body was lying and stood ramrod straight in front of the crying women. Sharada was the first to notice my arrival. She came up to me, put her arms around my neck and started weeping.

Then the death rites took their own course. The responsibility for binding Amma's mouth and hands with sections torn off from her old white sari was undertaken by Chittappa, who was an expert in such matters. Sharada's husband and other relatives were discussing ways to send word to our kith and kin. The Sambukars who had come to play the kottu were warming the leather faces of their drums over a fire. Under the shade of the banyan tree, the funeral hearse for Amma's final journey was being prepared. One of our women neighbours who was making coffee for those who came to pay their respects to the departed very kindly brought me a cup. Without shedding a single tear, I stood at the entrance, extending my hand towards the mourners who arrived in a steady stream. I became flustered when the women hugged me and wept. I could not match up to their grief.

Teachers and colleagues from the school came in a van. Even as they were asking me, 'Is Karunakaran Sir here already?', his ash-grey car glided to a halt in front of the house. Overcome by surprise, all eyes turned in my direction. To avoid seeing him, Sharada hid herself in the crowd of wailing women who had gathered in the veranda around Amma's corpse. Standing under the pandal, Karunakaran offered words of consolation to everyone in our family. I was in a state of panic, imagining the terrible consequences of an encounter between Karunakaran and Sharada. But Sharada claimed later that she had not seen him at all. 'I don't want to see his face as long as he is alive. If I must see him, I'll only see his corpse. It's in your hands,' she said in a hushed whisper, sitting on the string cot after the rites for the third day were over. Squatting on the ground, I listened to her.

When I went to that house later, I realized that the deadline I had set for wreaking vengeance on Karunakaran would expire in exactly two days. I felt weary. I wanted to quit my foolish fantasies about a vow that had tormented me all this while—one that I would never be able to fulfil—even if I had to bear the pain of failure. I stood in front of their house, determined to take their leave one last time. On seeing me, Sulo leapt with joy. 'Hey! So, you've come finally!' she greeted me in exhilaration and ran inside, almost shouting with excitement.

The family seemed to be getting ready for a celebration. Since the joyful atmosphere was making me even more depressed, I decided to leave immediately. I went to the office in search of Karunakaran, but he was not there. Asking the thin young man who could recite from one to hundred about Karunakaran's whereabouts, I made my way to the farm. Karunakaran was in the cattle shed with a group of workers. On seeing me, his kind eyes widened in surprise.

'Clerk Sir? Come! I was going to send for you myself,' he said and moved a couple of steps forward. 'So you're free now? All right, go home, get your stuff and come back. We are heading to Veerapur. Have you ever been to Veerapur? It's the site where the Kunnadaiya Sami legend took place. All the heads that were chopped off in battle are still lying there. All the blood spilled on the battlefield has congealed into stones. A visit will earn us merit in the hereafter. We'll be rid of all our evil afflictions. You've gone there, surely? Of course you have! How could anyone living here not have been to Veerapur?' He walked briskly while he continued talking. I was in a daze.

Sulo was running around in restless excitement. She had bathed, changed her clothes and worn what had become a personal marker—a string of pink-edged royal jasmine flowers in her hair. Now she was ordering everyone to hurry up and get ready. 'What, 'pa? You are coming with us, aren't you?' She winked at me. 'I agreed only because of you. We are going to stay there for two days. When you're there, I'll deal with you,' she said, wagging her index finger as if to threaten me.

When I reached the entrance, Gowthaman, who had arrived with his college friends, got out of the car. 'Welcome, Sir,' he greeted me and clasped my hands. He inquired in a solicitous manner about Amma and her final rites. Then he invited me to go to Veerapur with them and take part in the festivities. As if fearful that the smell of alcohol from his mouth would make me uncomfortable, he moved away in a hurry. His maturing physique had already begun to acquire a resemblance to his father's.

I joined them on the trip, considering it a miraculous opportunity to fulfil my vow. Karunakaran seemed incredibly cheerful. Like a young man, he kept up a lively banter with everyone all through the journey. I travelled with him for some time, then shifted to Gowthaman's car. Karunakaran's relatives and servants were following us in a truck loaded with tarpaulin sheets and ropes needed for erecting tents, and rams and roosters to be slaughtered for our meals, along with all the paraphernalia needed for cooking outdoors. After we crossed Karur, Sulo came over to our car. When she got into the back seat, I shifted to the front and sat next to the driver. Sulo's elderly uncle and aunt were sitting with her in the back. Gowthaman, who was at the wheel, whistled casually as he sped along. He chatted about cricket now and then. From the back seat, Sulo kept teasing me. Inserting her thin fingers through the gaps in the seats, she kept pinching my waist. Whenever I looked back, she would put on an innocent face and pretend to be gazing idly through the window. Afraid that I might drown in the secret pools of love brimming in her eyes, I began to panic.

Once we reached Veerapur, however, I tried to brace myself. After a round of wandering alone through the uncontrollable crowds at the festival, I returned to our tarpaulin tent. Families of servants who had been brought along were clearing the ground of grass, vegetation and dead leaves. The Pandarams were busy with their cooking chores. Sulo had gone traipsing in the woods with her friends and relatives. Impelled by foolish hopes, I went looking for her.

From among the dark-red stones strewn on the battlefield, Sulo had collected a few. Now she was setting them down on her mother's swollen knees. Throwing me a disdainful glance, she went over to her father, who was sitting in the shade of a wunja tree, and hid behind him. Her mother, who was massaging her swollen knees, called out to me. Pointing to the dark-red stones, she said, 'Will you collect a few of these and place them on my knees? These stones will cure my knees, they tell me. When I asked this girl, she set down one or two and ran away,' she said. Tracking Sulo with my eyes while she stood at a distance, talking to her father with her hands clutching a branch of the wunja tree, I tried to fulfil her mother's request. Enduring the unpleasant odour that rose from the older woman's body as she reclined with her sari pulled up, exposing her pale, bloodless thighs, I scooped up fistfuls of those hot stones and placed them on her swollen knees. Then I stood up and walked towards the temple. As I made my way through the crowd, looking idly at the stalls where sweets were arranged in stacks like temple towers, Sulo materialized suddenly at my side. In a flirtatious tone, she said, 'Hey, buy me a sweet, 'pa.' I wondered whether she had been following me all along.

I walked ahead through the press of the crowd with Sulo following behind. Since no one familiar seemed to be around, I brushed against her boldly as we walked. She held my hand. When I tried to free my hand, she withdrew hers. She bought a few sweets from a stall. Holding them in her hand, she whispered, 'It seems you are fawning on your mother-in-law. I was watching you. Keep at it, boy. She will support us in the future.' Then she pinched my waist fondly again and vanished. I roamed around for a long time, quite alone in that humongous crowd.

Folk singers had laid siege to the whole mountainside. The sound of udukkais came from all directions. The thousands of rams that had been brought there to be slaughtered were bleating constantly. Young men with false smiles were loitering behind the women. I set out to explore the woods where hopbush plants grew in abundance. I walked with aching feet along the arid trail that led first to Koovandam Valley, and from there to the top of Veeramalai Hill. In the woods populated by wunja trees, multiple card games were in progress. Plastic tumblers filled with country liquor by their side, a group of men played cards, making a raucous din. When they saw me, they stopped shouting for a moment and looked me over, then resumed their game with even greater gusto. People were collecting in plastic containers the murky water that flowed from a spring at the foot of the giant pongam tree in Koovandam Valley. Women were jostling one another to scoop the spring water in their palms, pour it into their mouths and sprinkle it on their heads. With great difficulty I cut through the crowd and had a peek at the spring. From the root of the pongam tree, water mixed with red soil gushed out with a growl as if from a municipal tap. Young men were filling up containers with spring water for women and the elderly. I asked one of them if I could get a bottle, and he offered me one immediately because I looked like a city dweller. I took it, intending to give it to Sulo or her mother, and moved on.

I couldn't spot so much as a small bird in the dense groves of hill-mango trees and thickets of spiral cactus on both sides of the trail. I thought the crowds might have pushed them to distant places. But an old man told me something surprising. 'This is the sacred truth, thambi. You won't come across a single crow, sparrow, dog or fox in this forest. Look at the number of goats slaughtered here and the amount of rice cooked, but you won't see a single crow.' With his words running through my mind, I walked towards the hilltop, scanning the entire forest with my eyes, searching for evidence to refute his claim. When I was halfway there, I saw a small patch of shade on a rock and rested my tired body on it. I began to think of possible ways to exact my revenge before this night of festivities passed. When I woke up, hearing the sound of udukkais from somewhere, I saw a troupe of itinerant singers trudging past. Like the destiny that was guiding me through life, the bard of Valanthankottai appeared before me, walking along with the group.

'Hey, maapillai! Seems like you've stretched out in the shade.' He came over to where I was relaxing and lit a beedi for himself. I picked up the udukkai he had set down and held it in my hands. When I pulled the string tight and tapped it lightly with my fingers, it went *bum*, *bum*, *bum*.

'So the government flunkey wants to learn how to sing?' the singer said, laughing. 'Since the job doesn't pay enough, he earns money from a rich family too,' he said in a hushed tone and winked at me. 'Are they paying you a good salary?' After he had asked me about the work I did in Karunakaran's house and my association with the family, he looked directly into my eyes. Unable to meet those wrinkled eyes, I looked away. Then he asked me about Sulo. He told me that rumours of a relationship between her and me were doing the rounds.

He then warned me with a note of concern. 'They are rich people. Don't get involved with her out of lust. It might seem like they've barely noticed but they'll finish you off quietly—knock you dead and throw you in the canal. No one will come out in support of people like us. When it's a matter of their caste-community, everyone—cousins, uncles, brothers-in-law—will band together. Who is there to speak up for a barber like you or me? "Look at that barber's cheek," they'll say but won't come forward to support you. We've seen it all. Don't even need to go far. As if you don't know the story of how the Kavundar scion from Kolathupalayam farmstead took my wife away and dumped her a month later on our doorstep, washing his hands of her. No one in the village stood up to seek justice for her. She felt so humiliated that she killed herself. Today, that

Kavundar owns a flashy car and goes around happily in it. And I've become a pauper. I carry this thing in my hand and go from village to village, singing a few songs and dancing a little so I get to eat some gruel every day.' After turning up the wick of vengeance burning in my heart, he picked up his udukkai and left.

Food was being prepared in the tents. The smell of meat was wafting from all directions. Women were grinding pepper and other condiments. With nothing to do, I wandered for some time through the narrow passages between the tents; then I went to a garden to the right of the temple. I could make out Gowthaman's head poking out from behind a bush. He was drinking with his friends. He smiled awkwardly on seeing me and stepped out from behind the bush. 'Will you have a drink, Sir? Just for a bit of fun, Sir,' he said, thrusting a bottle into my hands, and walked off hurriedly. Shoving the bottle into my trouser pocket, I went in search of the troubadour. I wandered for a long time, looking for him among the singers with painted faces who were rehearsing on several small stages erected around the temple. Finally, I found him with a group of men skinning the slaughtered goats. Though he was already drunk, he was happy to receive the bottle from me. After securing the knife soaked in goat blood at his waist, he scooped a handful of liver meat into a fold of his veshti and tied it in a bundle. Not knowing why, I followed him. Leading me to a dense part of the forest, he collected some twigs, lit a fire and roasted the liver meat. When he kept his blood-soaked knife on the ground, I was astonished to hear the secret call of destiny that had brought me there. In the blink of an eye, I had grabbed the knife and hidden it in my vest. I chatted with him until nightfall. As I was returning to the tent, I began to sweat profusely. I decided that I had to bring the chess game I was playing with Karunakaran to an end that very night. I dug a pit six inches deep under the lone vanni tree in the barren ground beyond the temple and buried the knife. As a marker, I arranged two or three granite slabs leaning one against another like a modern sculpture, and came back to the tent.

I couldn't say whether I had planned everything in advance. But these incidents which had begun to occur in a smooth and orderly sequence were making me nervous. The possibility of wreaking vengeance on Karunakaran before the expiry of my self-imposed deadline was turning into a certainty now. It felt as though I was being steered by someone else. I ran into Gowthaman and his friends in the market.

'Where did you go, Sir? My father's been looking for you. He told me that if I ran into you, I should ask you to meet him,' he said and hurried away.

This Karunakaran is inviting his fate of his own volition, I thought.

The tent was brimming over with joy and exhilaration. Suspended in a state of mild intoxication, the men were smiling secretly at women they wanted to possess. The women bantered and laughed, teased and made fun of one another, even as they were getting ready for secret revelries. When I saw Karunakaran sitting cross-legged at the centre of the tent, cleaning a double-barrelled rifle, I was flabbergasted. Sulo was looking on idly with the innocence of a child. Karunakaran smiled when he saw me. 'Clerk Sir, have your dinner. Let's go on a rabbit hunt,' he said. 'Veeramalai forest is piled high with rabbits. I never come here without a rifle. Though we slaughter many goats and chickens, I am never satisfied unless I shoot a few rabbits, roast them over a fire and eat a couple of pieces,' he said. I finished my dinner quickly and joined them. Sulo, who was sitting on a sack of rice in front of me as I ate, boring into me with her pink-edged gaze, wanted to convey something to me with her bashful eyes. I even wondered whether she might have an inkling about my secret plan for revenge. But I was in raptures thinking of the impending rabbit hunt and the double-barrelled rifle in Karunakaran's hands. The rifle had triggered fantasies of daring adventure. My storyline was turning into something completely unexpected. But I was disappointed when Karunakaran's barber and a Nadar youth set out along with us.

As his hunting ground, Karunakaran had chosen the fields to the north-east of the temple, with standing crops of ragi and sorghum. He had strapped a hunter's lamp, capable of producing a bright and narrow beam of light, to his forehead. The other two men were holding a flashlight each. Everyone carried a thick club as well. One of the men gave me a wunja stick to carry for personal security. He also had a catapult hanging from his shoulder. The other man had an empty gunnysack draped over his shoulder. I wrapped a shawl around myself.

Just then the troubadours started playing their udukkais to attract listeners. When we passed through the market, that other man concealed the rifle inside his gunnysack. Women and children were jostling one another in shops that sold dolls and bangles. Even though a sizeable crowd had gathered, the carousel operators were still calling out to everyone.

Telling them I had to pee, I went to the barren ground, retrieved the knife buried under the vanni tree and tucked it at my waist. I wrapped the shawl tightly around myself and walked back. We remained silent until we had travelled beyond the reach of the sounds and lights of the festivities. I walked behind them. Karunakaran kept talking in a low voice about the finer points of hunting and the way a man must conduct himself on the hunting ground. He advised me to follow the footsteps of the hunter and walk behind him.

As soon as a rabbit was spotted, the hunter would take aim. Everyone else would need to stay where they were, without moving. It was important to follow this rule.

After we had crossed a certain distance, the lamp fixed on Karunakaran's forehead was turned on. Its pointed beam began to move very slowly across the swaying sorghum stalks at a height of six inches. We followed him in absolute silence. The horn suspended from his shoulder kept making a chirping sound like crickets. When the light passed a fence, we spotted a rabbit. Cautioning us in a low whisper, Karunakaran advanced furtively, keeping himself hidden. Frightened, the rabbit leapt into the field. Refusing to turn its face to the ring of light that followed in malevolent pursuit, it crossed the field successfully, ran towards the south and disappeared.

'A proper tease. See how it simply wouldn't make eye contact?' said Karunakaran wearily and lit a cigarette. Ordering everyone to follow him quietly, he walked ahead, pointing the beam of the flashlight towards the ground. With the lamp on his forehead turned off, the hillocks appeared tall as dark silhouettes in the mellow light of the stars. After walking for ten minutes, he switched on his lamp again; in the third minute, we spotted a pair of eyes glinting brightly in the distance. Our bodies turned rigid and still. Karunakaran took aim. Standing hidden behind the others, I saw those glinting eyes with my heart pounding. The trigger being pulled, the bullet exploding and the wounded rabbit leaping and falling had happened in the same instant. 'Sister-fucker trying to pull its tricks on me!' he muttered as he walked towards the fallen rabbit.

The rabbit was dead by then. Karunakaran's barber stuffed its carcass into the gunnysack.

During the next one hour, we did not spot a single creature. I was exhausted from trudging endlessly through the woods. 'Can't see a single piece today. Maybe some fellow has come and wiped them out totally,' Karunakaran lamented as he walked ahead. Suddenly a viper snake appeared on the foot trail, blocking it. When we looked up after we had pummelled it to death, we realized that Karunakaran had spotted a pair of rabbits. Instructing us to be quiet, he went ahead alone. Holding our breath, we stood still and watched the lamp's beam as it scanned the surroundings at an unhurried pace. After advancing steadily for some time, the light darted here and there and came to a halt at a particular spot. When we heard the bullets leaving the rifle with an angry hiss, we ran in that direction. Karunakaran was turning over the body of the wounded rabbit. In the next ten minutes, he also hunted down the rabbit that had got away. Every now and then, he would hand over the flashlight, lamp and rifle to the young Nadar and talk to me as we walked together.

I was waiting for the right moment to tear Karunakaran's body apart with the knife drenched in the blood of my vengeance. The gunnysack was filled with the carcasses of dead rabbits. I felt sorry for Karunakaran's barber as he staggered along, weighed down by this intolerable burden. After midnight, all of us halted in a peasant's hut in the middle of the forest, intending to rest there for a short while. Totally exhausted by now, Karunakaran lay supine on the floor. The other two dumped the rabbits on the ground and tried to count them in the light of the hunter's lamp. Then, after whispering conspiratorially to each other, they got up and went into the forest. I was left alone with Karunakaran. His eyes were already glazed over with sleep.

I imagined that, clutching his rifle tight, he was watching me with his sleepy eyes. Since the moment of fulfilling my vow was close, my body began to shiver and tremble. I remembered Sharada's brown eyes. Ignoring fantasies about Sulo's pink-edged love, I gripped the handle of the blood-soaked knife that I had kept hidden at my waist. My hands were shaking. That night of festivities was quietly gliding past these crucial minutes that were about to overturn Karunakaran's fate as well as mine. However, as if a man, or a wild animal, or a small but dangerous creature of the forest, or something else altogether, had got in my way, I remained passive and immobile, staring at my enemy as though I was trying to make sure that it was really him. I wondered if it was cowardice. Whether out of cowardice or mercy, I let that wonderful opportunity slip by and stood perfectly still as if paralysed.

After a long time, the barber and the young Nadar who had gone into the forest with him came back. Karunakaran woke up only after their return. 'You could have had a short nap, couldn't you?' he asked me with concern and stretched to ease his limbs. 'How many pieces, da?' he asked the men about the rabbits. 'All right, shall we leave? We can go and listen to the recital for a bit. They have yet to perform the song about marking and staging the battlefield,' he said as though he was talking to himself, and got up. Quietly, I dropped the blood-soaked knife right there and, feeling terribly humiliated, I followed those three bodies that had begun to walk enthusiastically towards the tent, unaware of anything that I had gone through only a short while ago.

There was no one in the tent. Everyone must have gone to listen to the recital. The spiteful roll of the udukkais filled the tent and passed into the night. The two men left for the woods to clean the dead rabbits, and Karunakaran and I were left alone again. Since that didn't strike my weary brain as important in any way, I spread a sheet in a dark corner of the tent and stretched my tired body on it. After washing his face, hands and feet and changing into new clothes, Karunakaran invited me to go with him to hear the performance of the troubadours. I told him I had a headache and stayed put.

I was afraid that the veins in my forehead might burst open. I wondered if I should slip away immediately. I wanted to confess my failure to Sharada and advise her to forget about the past as a bad dream and continue her peaceful life in the present. I felt she might laugh at the idea. Not wanting to think about these things any more, I pulled up the sheet and covered myself. The troubadours were approaching the final stages of the story. I was afraid that the cadence of the udukkais that was coming in from all directions might make me lose my mind. That I could not leave the forest without a vehicle was scarier than anything else. A memory of Sulo surfaced out of the blue in my mind. Wanting to escape from it, I tried to sleep. Before I lost consciousness completely, Sulo appeared like a curse in my dream. The fragrance of pink-edged royal jasmine began to caress my nostrils. I wondered if the reason I had let go of the opportunity to take revenge on Karunakaran was my love for Sulo. I was overcome by revulsion at myself. I tried to fling the sheet aside and get up. Sulo was sitting very close to me. I thought it could be a residual image from the dream.

'That's why I wanted to tell you not to go there,' she whispered and bent down towards me.

When she stroked my forehead with her cool hand, I realized that it wasn't a dream. I held her hand. She was wearing a set of pink glass bangles. I caressed them gently. 'I bought them in the shop next to the temple car,' she said and tried to free her hand from mine. My grip had turned urgent. 'Let go! You'll break the bangles,' she said. Fear began to spread in her eyes. I sprang to my feet and held her in a tight embrace. She was shocked and tried to shake me off. As if by a premeditated move, I tried to kindle her emotions. She was panting. Her body had grown limp.

Her eyes had rolled back into her head. She lay down on her back. I spread over her body. 'No, 'pa,' she whimpered in a feeble voice. Meanwhile, I had brought her soft body, which had turned dry and brown from the unbearable heat of love, under my control. I grabbed her breasts, which were like two upturned yellow chrysanthemums, in a spiteful frenzy of revenge. Sulo tried to scream. I pressed my lips down on hers to stifle the sound. Then, without any interruption, I filled her body with the viscous fluid of vengeance that brimmed over within me. I got up, lit a cigarette and came to the well-lit front portion of the tent, checking to see whether anyone was around.

Sulo was sobbing. My ears had turned numb. Then I felt the warmth of her body, shaking like a squirrel, on my back. Like a frightened child, Sulo clung to me with her arms around my neck. 'Why did you do this to me before my wedding?' she mumbled pathetically in a broken voice. I was trying to recall Sharada's brown eyes. It was at that exact moment—when I was distraught, unable to meet the eyes of that young girl who was yearning to be consoled by me, powerless to smooth away the hair that clung to her sweaty face, not brave enough to plant a gentle kiss on her bruised cheeks—I heard that terrible cry.

I had begun to wail as if I had been engulfed by a great sin. Just then, a woman's voice that seemed intimately familiar started descending like a curse on that night of festivities. As if she had recognized it, an agitated Sulo shoved me aside and ran. I stumbled and collapsed on the floor. I lay there for a long time, listening to the sounds of her heels as they receded and eventually died down. Until the briny smell of her tears had faded away completely and disappeared like vapour, I could not regain consciousness. Then, like a diffident snail, I stepped out of the tent.

There were signs that chaos had broken out on the battlefield. As if in obedience to someone's command, all the troubadours flung their udukkais away and ran in the direction from which the scream was heard. Thinking that it might be part of the story, the spectators turned their necks to watch them. Then, shocked at the news that was relayed to them in a loud voice, they too started to run behind the troubadours. The udukkais that were stamped on were moaning, unable to bear the pain. I joined the teeming crowd and was carried along with it in a direction I could scarcely see. A short distance away, I heard the loud wails of a young woman. Since they sounded like Sulo's, I forced my way through the crowd and forged ahead. There, surrounded by eager spectators who had gathered around him in a circle, like the central dot of that circle, like the character in the last scene of a play who was responsible for bringing it to an end, I saw Gowthaman standing with a blood-soaked knife in his hand. Crimson-yellow light from the tower of the Kandiyamman temple covered him like a curtain. Like a secondary character with no lines to speak, Karunakaran stood next to his son, his face white as a sheet.

Sulo's mother rolled around in grief on the barren ground. Sulo tried to pull her up and make her stand, and hold her in her arms. Sulo's crying sounded very faint, like melancholy background music, as though it was trying to fill the vacuum created by the sudden silence of the udukkais. As soon as he saw me, Gowthaman, who had been staring vacantly at the blood streaming from the two bodies that lay crumpled at his feet, let the knife slip from his hand and came running to me like someone begging for shelter.

~

EVENTUALLY, SOME OTHERS STEERED THIS story of my vengeance, people who had no connection with it.

Even I, who was very close to them, could not fully comprehend what had happened to Karunakaran and his family, or what awaited them in the future. After the incident, or right from the moment of its occurrence, Karunakaran's empire began to collapse like a house of cards. Charged with the murder of two of his college mates, Karunakaran's beloved son was arrested and sent to jail. Many rumours were in circulation about the reason for the murders. Someone claimed that it had to do with a woman. The father of one of the victims was a famous lawyer. The other was the son of an MLA who wielded far more power and influence than Karunakaran. The two fathers had joined hands in their efforts to seek retribution.

Since their relatives and the party with which Karunakaran was affiliated stood united in support of the victims, Karunakaran could hardly do anything to save his son.

Having lost all its prestige overnight, the family was stranded without help. Sleazy, concocted stories about Karunakaran and his family began to appear in the newspapers. His wife, who had always relished being a chronic patient, was truly afflicted now. Karunakaran was wandering around like a man unhinged. He spent lavish amounts on lawyers, paying them several times more money than they asked for, pleading with them to save his son somehow. No one came forward to help him. The ministers, upon whom he had once doted, refused to meet him. I observed everything from close quarters. By way of providing support to my enemy who had totally lost his equilibrium, I made endless visits to the courts, the prison complex where Gowthaman was incarcerated and lawyers' offices. From a distance, Sharada's brown eyes were watching everything with undiminished ill will. She spoke to me every day without fail. She pestered me to tell her in minute detail everything that had happened in Veerapur on that fateful day, and all that was happening now in its aftermath. I could sense the fervour of her sighs through the telephone receiver in my hand. She was worried that Karunakaran might come out unscathed from the crises that besieged him. When I explained logically that there was no chance of that happening, she was somewhat appeased. She was confident that the vengeful deities to whom she prayed would not forsake her. 'There's a lot more to come. You've been watching from up close, haven't you? Our Masani Amman will ruin that family. She will make them beg on the streets,' she said—as she did every time she brought her spiteful conversation to an end.

I had nothing to say to Sulo. Stung by the ignominy, she had discontinued her studies. She could scarcely believe what had happened to her family. Having lost her confidence as well as her innocence, she was becoming an extremely fragile girl who was in constant need of consolation and protection. I had no option but to provide her unwavering support in managing the household and arranging medical treatment for her mother. Later, everything became a matter of routine. Except Karunakaran, all the other members of the family were trying to preserve a semblance of normalcy in their lives even as they grappled with the horrible reality of their situation. Lost in fantasies of staging a full recovery from all his problems, Karunakaran had begun to renounce everything that belonged to him. Pretending to offer help, I moved around freely in that house which had been forsaken by friends and relatives. Like a ghoul, I was set on taking over all their private spaces.

'We would have felt like orphans without you. Thanks, 'pa,' Sulo would say. Whenever she got a chance, she expressed her gratitude through kisses. We kissed each other everywhere—in the kitchen, the office room, the cattle shed and the farmhouse. Sometimes we even got the opportunity to have sex. On those occasions, Sulo was shy and diffident. With no one to keep watch over us, I took advantage of her without any sense of guilt. 'You won't deceive me, will you?' She would elicit a promise from me after every kiss. I made plenty of false-hearted promises. When she told me one day that she was pregnant, I was stunned. I bought pills to induce an abortion and gave them to her but she refused to take them. 'No need, 'pa. Let it be. I want to cuddle your baby,' she said. She was adamant in her refusal to understand the horror of the situation. Then she calmed down within a couple of days. After extracting a promise from me as usual, she agreed to take the pills.

Completely in the dark about any of these goings-on, Karunakaran spent every waking minute looking for ways to resolve the crises that had engulfed him. He had given up his businesses one by one. The stone quarry was shut down. He withdrew his investments in various finance companies and spent the money to fight his son's case. When Gowthaman, who was released on bail after four months, was forced to live in a distant city as per his bail conditions, all of us made countless trips to see him. On some days, Karunakaran or I had to stay back in that city to keep him company. I took Sulo and her mother two or three times to visit him. Gowthaman appeared cheerful, firmly believing that he would be acquitted somehow and set free. Solid evidence and clear testimonies from several witnesses militated against his belief. It was in fact very likely that the trial court would hand him the death sentence. The lawyer kept warning me about it discreetly. Karunakaran knew it too. When I reported to him what the lawyer had advised me—in the event of a death sentence, we would need to approach the High Court and the Supreme Court—Karunakaran asked me not to mention it to Sulo or her mother.

He was being punished in ways more horrible than Sharada or I could ever have imagined. But we may have to wait for a long time before the last sentence of this story is written, I thought. Yet, apart from claiming credit for what someone else had done, what part could I or Sharada have played in this story? We could, if we wanted to, reveal to him who we were. We could remind him of the horrible incident that had taken place in his loan shop thirty years ago. I wondered whether I continued to stay with them only in anticipation of that moment.

Karunakaran wanted to save at least his darling daughter even as his family was experiencing a steep decline. After the charges were proved in the Sessions Court and Gowthaman was awarded the life sentence on two counts, everyone in the family was shattered. More than anyone else, it was Gowthaman who appeared to have lost all hope. While steps were being taken to appeal the decision in the High Court, Gowthaman, who was unable to get bail, was lodged in Central Jail. Without worrying about himself, he pleaded with everyone to arrange his sister's wedding by any means.

Later, Karunakaran consulted me about Sulo's marriage.

I pretended to encourage the initiative. I introduced marriage brokers of my acquaintance to the family. Karunakaran did not have too many options to choose from. When a distant relative without much education or wealth came forward to marry Sulo, Karunakaran was forced to accept the proposal with gratitude. I was somewhat familiar with the boy as he was once employed as a tractor operator in Karunakaran's stone quarry. At Karunakaran's request, I travelled fifteen miles to the boy's village and spoke to his widowed mother. Karunakaran's loyal family barber had come along too. Like rainwater filling up a river during torrential rain, greed inundated the old woman's eyes. She showed keen interest in learning about Karunakaran's properties. After several oblique questions, she came straight to the point. When I told her that I didn't have clear answers to her questions, she started being curt with me. Throughout our conversation, she tried relentlessly to project herself as a large-hearted person.

'We don't want his property and possessions. I thought the alliance would be like lending a hand to a man in trouble. I told the broker, "All right, let's go ahead." Our relatives are still against it. There are all kinds of rumours about that girl Sulo. I heard that her habits and lifestyle are unseemly. Never mind. Let people say what they like. I saw this as god's will and gave my consent. Does that mean we should accept her with no dowry at all? Once we do something that might antagonize our family circle, and tomorrow there's no one to help us in a crisis, we'll need resources to handle that situation, won't we?' she said shrewdly. Later, she asked me about the charges against Gowthaman and the chances of his acquittal and release. I tried to explain everything to her.

'It's going to cost a lot, eh?' she said. Then she started to worry about it. 'Why should we spend all that money and bring him out of jail? Let him serve his sentence and come out. As you say, they will surely have to let him out after, what, thirteen or fourteen years? Unless we have some money at that point, how will we get by? The way it's going, his father will give all his money to the lawyers and the police, and die in the end. How can the boy come out and live like a pauper? That's why I am telling you to go easy on the money. Otherwise, what are we going to do with his property?' She expressed her greed without a hint of shame. Later, when she got a chance to speak directly to Karunakaran, she was adamant that half his property should be made over to her son. In the presence of a handful of relatives who took part in the negotiations, Karunakaran acceded to her request right away.

When she heard about it, an outraged Sulo came looking for me. I was alone in Karunakaran's office which had fallen into disuse.

'Is Appa trying to get rid of me by giving away everything he has in the world? And you are helping him, aren't you?' she said. 'Forget about Appa. He doesn't know anything. In his present condition, he won't be able to think any differently. But aren't you ashamed of yourself? Why are you negotiating like a marriage broker? Are you greedy for the commission?' she lashed out at me.

I stayed silent, offering no response.

'Tell me, 'pa!' She grabbed me by the shoulders, shaking me. Then she broke down and began to weep. As if seeking refuge, she tried to lean on my shoulder. I stood up in alarm. Reminding me of her love and the promises I made whenever we kissed, she begged me to rescue her somehow from this crisis. Sobbing, she said that she could not think of a life without me, and wanted to know if I was afraid of her father and relatives. Finally suggesting that we go someplace far away, out of everyone's sight, get married and pursue our lives, she waited for my response. I couldn't bear to look at her teary eyes and tried to move away. Trying to stop me with her slender arms, she asked me to give her a final answer and looked deep into my eyes. I think the fakery visible in my eyes or the trickery evident in my manner must have conveyed something to her. Suddenly, she seemed to lose all hope. Her body began to shake. Shoving me aside, she said quietly, 'You have proved yourself to be just another average man. Thanks, 'pa.' Then she disappeared from there.

I wondered if I too had turned into someone like Karunakaran. But I had no wish to set anything right. After I returned home, I sat drinking through the night. In the morning, I went to meet Sharada. She was waiting eagerly to find out how far this story of vengeance had progressed. Ignoring other aspects, I began to tell her for the first time about Sulo, our love affair and my feelings of guilt. She listened to everything I said as though she were listening to a gripping episode.

'This is something I expected,' she said in a detached tone and sat in silence for a long time. Then she prepared coffee for the both of us. I thought she was trying not to believe what I had told her or to understand it in a different way.

'That Masani Amman will not let his family live in peace. I know that,' she expressed with finality a sentiment that was completely inappropriate for the occasion. 'Don't change your mind,' she warned me, wagging her finger. Then, after she had set down the coffee cup before me, she began to recount in a quiet voice everything that had happened—the story of our revenge from the beginning up to now. I felt suffocated. Since I had nothing at all to say to her, I took her leave and came out.

I stayed put at home for the next two days. Confident that Sulo would call me, I kept the receiver within arm's reach. In this story that was being steered by someone else, I was dreaming even then that something good might happen suddenly. Then, without any forethought, I went and stood in front of their house.

After a long time, that house was in a festive mood. Karunakaran told me that he had conducted Sulo's engagement with a simple ceremony just two days earlier, and he was sorry he could not invite me. Then he took me by the hand and led me inside. Sulo was standing in the hall with a numb expression. She greeted me as if nothing was amiss. As though she was offering the sweets and snacks prepared for a hastily arranged engagement ceremony to a total stranger, she brought a tray of eats, placed it before me calmly and continued to stand there. How else could she have behaved, I wondered.

'I am still quite strong and spirited. Tell me, can people understand that even when an elephant lies down, it is still taller than a horse? You'll see whether I conduct this girl's marriage with pomp and ceremony or not. I was surprised that this boy had suddenly got himself into trouble. He wasn't a loafer who roamed around carrying a knife, was he? Let people say a thousand things. I won't give up on him. It doesn't matter even if I lose everything I have but I won't rest until I get him out of jail. The lawyer has told me that even if the High Court lets us down, we can go to the Supreme Court and take the case apart. I want to get this girl settled properly first, then I'll swing into action.' Karunakaran talked as though he was throwing a challenge at someone. As if she had no interest in anything, Sulo moved away. I felt alienated from them suddenly.

But true to his word, Karunakaran conducted a grand wedding. Except on a couple of occasions, I did not participate in the wedding arrangements. Karunakaran had succeeded somehow in enlisting the cooperation of a few of his estranged relatives. Whenever his new relatives happened to see me, he was very particular about introducing me as the clerk in his office. When he introduced me once to a relative on the groom's side as 'our office clerk', I felt humiliated. Embarrassed at the change in my expression, he tried to make amends. He told them with evident pride, 'But he is like family. Without his help, I would've had a very hard time these past two years. He runs around day and night, dealing with the courts and the police. When kith and kin have abandoned us, he is standing by our side. See how hard he is working for Sulochana's wedding, like a brother.' I couldn't stand it, but I understood the self-protective intent behind the description 'like a brother', and smiled sheepishly.

Sulo had become close to her mother-in-law well ahead of the marriage, or perhaps she pretended to be. I thought she was trying to make me jealous. But I understood rather belatedly that she only wanted to humiliate me. She had become audacious enough to order me around in front of her relatives. I remained submissive without offering any resistance. She couldn't have doubted that I would submit to her. In the end, both of us grew tired of this game. Suddenly one day, I stopped going to their house.

A week before the wedding, their family barber came looking for me. Since I was still hoping that her marriage might be cancelled due to some unforeseen intervention, I was excited by his visit. When I learnt that Karunakaran had sent him to formally present the wedding invitation to me, I felt let down. The man told me that Karunakaran was heartbroken. The tractor operator is not a suitable match for Sulo, he added. Knowing that he expected me to say something, I remained silent.

Two days later, I visited their house at Karunakaran's invitation. He had bought a shirt and a pair of trousers for me. 'I should have done more for you but it was a bad time,' he said with a sigh. Then he insisted that I should come to the wedding hall two days before the function. 'Though Gowthaman is eligible for parole to attend the wedding, he doesn't want to,' Karunakaran told me with an almost inaudible sob. 'I think it's a good decision. If he turns up, it will mean unnecessary trouble for everyone. If someone says something nasty, we can't keep quiet and there'll be trouble. I am wondering whether I should take Sulo along and visit him after two days,' he said. Expecting that he would invite me to come along with him to see Gowthaman, I remained silent. Karunakaran was smoking incessantly. Both of us were becoming hard-hearted. During the two hours I spent there, Sulo was not to be seen at all. I wondered whether I should ask him. I thought she might have gone to present the wedding invitation to a friend. I couldn't believe that she would be in a frame of mind to do that. Then, since it suddenly seemed as if it was all over, I excused myself and returned home.

Like an outsider, I went to the wedding hall during the auspicious window when the main wedding rituals were performed, and stood with my office colleagues and teachers who had come to attend the function. Afterwards, we went as a group to convey our felicitations to the newly-weds who were seated on the stage. Sulo greeted everyone with a smile. As I passed her, she whispered something in the tractor operator's ear.

A large number of relatives and friends had come to the wedding. When I came out of the hall, Karunakaran's wife, who was sitting near the entrance in a wheelchair, called me by my name. Saying that she was very happy that I could attend, she made me sit on a plastic chair in front of her and chatted with me for some time. Suddenly, as if she remembered just then, she asked me whether I had enjoyed the wedding feast. Noting the delay in my response, she sent for a girl from the hall and instructed her to take me inside and make sure that I ate. Not satisfied with that, she followed me in her wheelchair, entered the dining hall and sat next to me. Following the meal, she presented a gift bag to me with her kind hands, and only then did she permit me to leave.

After Sulo's wedding, I stopped going to Karunakaran's house altogether. To extricate myself from everything, I applied for a transfer. I took a long break from work and went from town to town like a nomad, meeting old friends. I made a few attempts to reunite my younger sister with her husband, but they ended in failure. Just when a layer of ash was beginning to shroud my bitter memories, out of the blue I received a call from Karunakaran's house. It was my younger sister, a character of no importance in this story, who had received Sulo's call. By my sister's account, Sulo had asked me to contact her immediately, her tone had been somewhat anxious and she had disconnected the call in a hurry.

'Call her back. Poor thing, she seems to be in some trouble,' my sister said. 'I'll take care of it later,' I told her. Then I went to the market and called Karunakaran's residence from a public telephone. The phone kept ringing. Thinking that the very special moment I had been waiting for had finally arrived, I went to their house. The house was deserted and looked as though it had been abandoned. Sensing that someone was moving about in the passage beyond the wide-open front door, I stepped in nervously. I saw Karunakaran's family barber with another woman.

'Sir, come in. Our Kavundar has been admitted to the hospital. Didn't you get the news?'

'What happened?'

'He fainted and collapsed suddenly. There was no one at home. I came to know only when Pazhana told me. It happened the day before yesterday, between nine and nine-thirty at night. Pazhanichami rushed out and brought a doctor. "His blood pressure has gone way up; take him to Coimbatore immediately," the doctor said. Then, after informing Chinna Kavundachi by phone, Paraman and I hired a car and took him straight to KG Hospital. Sometime later, Chinna Kavundachi came there. Poor thing, she couldn't withstand the strain. She is eight months gone now. She might have phoned you. Were you out of town or something?'

I left as soon as I could. An ineffable happiness began to flood my heart. Before leaving, I went to Karunakaran's office, which was covered in garbage and filth, and informed Sharada on the telephone. It was a bus journey of nearly two hours to Coimbatore. Indulging myself in fantasies of an emotional meeting with Sulochana, with me consoling her gently, I huddled uncomfortably in my seat and fell asleep. Unable to endure dreams filled with hazy images and bewildering sounds, I woke up within ten minutes. Suddenly, I wondered whether this might be a pointless trip.

I spotted Sulo and that former tractor operator who was her husband at the entrance of the hospital. Assuming that they had been waiting for me, I started explaining to them in an apologetic tone why I could not visit them in the past few weeks. Sulo said that they were on their way to a nearby eatery for breakfast. She mentioned the number of the ward where Karunakaran was admitted and asked me to go there. I suspected that she was trying to present me to her husband as a servant of the family. I decided against obeying her instruction and walked out of the hospital compound. Standing near a pavement stall opposite the railway station, I lit a cigarette. Sulo, who was following her husband with her fully distended belly, had noticed me. Her scornful eyes moved away instantly. When I went back to the ward, Sulo had already returned from the eatery. I had assumed that they were helpless and waiting for my support and assistance; instead, I found many of their relatives sitting on chairs outside the patient's room. Since no one was permitted to see the patient, they were seeking information from Sulo and her husband. In a hushed voice, Sulo was giving them brief answers.

When I tried to talk to her, Sulo rebuffed me and went into the patient's room. She was trying to tell me that I was not important to her any more. To conceal my disappointment, I started chatting with her husband, who was standing outside with no one to pay him attention. He pretended not to know anything about me. He told me that one of his relatives was working as a teacher in my school and asked me if I knew that person.

When she came out of the patient's room, Sulo was irritated to see the two of us sitting next to each other, engaged in a conversation. Handing him the prescription she was carrying, she bade him to go to the dispensary in the basement and buy the medicines. I went along with him. All the way there and back, he bragged endlessly about the status and prestige of his family. I guessed that most of it must have been his imagination. He also told me that Sulo was not fit to be his wife and he had consented to the marriage only because of Karunakaran's kindness of heart. He asked me not to repeat any of this to Sulo. I thought he was a pathetic creature.

Most of the visitors had left before dusk. Sulo's husband began to worry about the cattle on his farm. 'You can never trust the servants,' he said. For Sulo, who was nearing full-term in her pregnancy, the hospital was a place of acute discomfort. Reckoning all these factors, I seemed to be the only one who could stay with Karunakaran round-the-clock. Over the next two days, until Karunakaran was transferred from the Intensive Care Unit to a normal ward, I was so busy that I barely had time to breathe. Then her husband said that he had to go to his village urgently and prepared to leave.

'If necessary, I'll send Amma,' he said, trying to appease an angry Sulo. That night, as Sulo slept on the extra bed in the patient's room, I went to the visitors' hall in the basement, leaned back in one of the chairs and rested for some time. Sulo called me just after midnight and once again at dawn: the first time to collect test reports from the lab and the second, to bring her coffee. I obeyed her instructions without demur. The next morning, after ordering me to bring her breakfast, she offered me some money for my expenses. I declined. She was furious.

'No one has to do us any favours for free,' she said.

'I am not a servant working for a wage,' I replied curtly, and she looked up at me.

'It's not as if we don't know who will ask for what wage,' she said and closed her eyes. Completely shattered, I took the money and hurried away.

I was able to give Sharada plenty of good news. When I told her that Karunakaran's condition didn't leave much room for hope, she asked me in a spiteful tone, 'Is he likely to die soon?'

'Not immediately,' I said, 'but it will be difficult for him to get up and walk again. One side is completely paralysed.'

'Then he will pee and shit in bed, you say?'

I remained silent.

'He shouldn't die immediately. As punishment for all his sins, he should remain bedridden for at least two or three years, and have maggots crawling all over his body before he dies eventually. He must have ruined so many lives! The wealth he has amassed by robbing the poor—it won't be spent on anything worthy or decent. God knows how many must have cursed him, just like me.' Sharada spoke with such hatred and vehemence that she was panting.

Karunakaran needed many tests for which he had to be taken to different departments of the hospital. We had to keep transferring his paralysed body from the bed to stretchers, from stretchers to wheelchairs, and from wheelchairs to scanners. Sulo's husband and mother-in-law assisted me by turns. Sulo stayed nights in the hospital as the main caregiver for her father. I went home once every two or three days. Her mother-in-law was watching me the whole time with hostile intent. She asked many subtle questions with the aim of finding out my caste and how I was connected to the family. Since she did not get a clear answer from Sulo, she asked me directly. Her face lit up after I told her my grandfather's name.

'You are Kumara Nasuvan's grandson, are you? The old man who reads horoscopes? Is he your maternal or paternal grandfather? Is Kumaran still alive? He must be very old now.'

I was being insulted by a member of that family for the first time. Sulo looked on with chagrin as I turned red in the face.

'Is your mother doing all right? Silamba is her name, right?'

'That's my mother's older sister.'

'Oh yes. Your mother's name is Mutha, I remember now. She said she was living near Mayilrangam in the south, in Udayampalayam or Nachipalayam.' Then she recounted the entire history of our family.

'When your father was a teacher in Kannammapuram, he used to come to our house. His family faced a lot of hardship then. They had to scrounge even for food. My father took pity on him and helped him out now and then. What are you doing now? Working as a farmhand here, is it?'

When I told her that I was employed in a government school, she was astonished.

'Not bad. You used to sell murukku in the tent cinema in Arasalur. I've seen you there myself. You went to school after that, did you?'

My body began to tremble at this intolerable humiliation. To blink back the tears that filled my eyes, I rushed to the bathroom and washed my face. When I came back, Sulo was saying something to her mother-in-law in a low whisper.

I left immediately. I roamed the congested roads and railway-station platforms of that apathetic city for a long time. Then I went to a bar, drank a little whisky, and stopped at a municipality park where I watched idly as lovers exchanged furtive kisses in secluded corners. I tried to think. The absurdity of my having entered Karunakaran's household with fantasies of exacting revenge and ending up as one of their pathetic farmhands surviving on their mercy was intolerable to me. I stood up, intending to return at once to the hospital, collect my clothes and leave without informing anyone. As I passed under a canopy of creepers, a part-time prostitute with big breasts beckoned me. When I tried to ignore her and move on, she muttered a horrible expletive at me. On my way to the hospital in a highly perturbed state, I spotted that former tractor operator. He was carrying a big suitcase.

'How are you, Sir? You seem very tired,' he inquired with concern. I walked on without a word. I felt that instead of departing as a jilted lover and a disgraced man, I might as well wreak vengeance on them. I wondered spitefully whether I should talk to this man about the relations I had enjoyed with Sulo.

Sulo was fast asleep. Her mother-in-law, who was chatting with a middle-aged woman from the next room, left her abruptly and came over to us. After asking her son about household matters, including the health of their cattle, she started telling him the secrets she had unearthed about me.

'Do you know who he is, Sambu? He is our Kumara Nasuvan's grandson. Didn't you know the old man? He came to our house five or six times. He was the one who cast your horoscope.'

Sulo, who had been roused awake by the voices, looked flustered. She tried to intervene. Perhaps trying to change the subject, she began to tell her husband what the doctor had said about Karunakaran's condition. 'He says a clot has formed in the brain. If they perform an operation, there is an eighty per cent chance that it will be cured. If the operation fails, his survival will be at risk. I was waiting for you to come back.' The former tractor operator blinked uncomprehendingly like an idiot. Then she said with an air of finality, 'We should tell them there is no need for an operation. Even if he is permanently bedridden, we will at least get to see him alive for a few more years, no? That's enough. If they operate on him and something happens, what will I do, given the mess our family is in?' She sobbed. Hearing her sobs, Karunakaran woke up and whimpered. She wiped her eyes quickly and went to him.

'When are they going to discharge him?' her husband asked me as we left the room. We stood near the gates of the cinema hall next to the hospital and chatted for some time. Before long, he had begun to gaze aimlessly at the street.

Sulo decided to get Karunakaran discharged in the next two days and take him home. I ran around to settle hospital bills, buy the prescribed medicines and procure the equipment needed for physiotherapy. Her mother-in-law watched with unease whenever Sulo and I happened to speak to each other. At one stage, she even intervened. She didn't like the way Sulo addressed me. 'Why do you keep calling him "Sir"? Is he a stranger? Just a Nasuvan boy from our village, right? If you call him "Sir", what will our caste-community think?' I tried to retaliate but Sulo looked at me pleadingly. Then she chastised her mother-in-law herself.

'What's wrong with you, talking to an educated man about his caste? Won't you keep quiet for even a minute?' After admonishing her mother-in-law sternly, Sulo apologized to me for the old woman's behaviour.

'Sorry, Sir. She is old-fashioned,' she said.

Nurturing fantasies of revenge, I put up with Sulo's rebuffs and her mother-in-law's barbs. To protect my self-respect, I did not eat a morsel in their house. Sulo decided to stay on in her father's house. On the pretext of looking after the land that still remained with them, her husband stayed back with her. Karunakaran had gradually learned to live with his condition. Now he was able to enunciate a couple of words with great difficulty and make a few gestures with his left hand. That Karunakaran had to rely on his wheelchair to move around was a source of immense grief to his wife. Sulo was the only person in that house who reposed complete trust in me. Despite my intentions with regard to Karunakaran, I had begun to feel sorry for Sulo.

I took charge of all court-related matters. For every expense that I incurred, I submitted accounts to Sulo's mother-in-law. She kept insulting me as usual. I wanted Sulo to witness it and be hurt by it. The old woman was focused on protecting what remained of Karunakaran's properties. To her naive and foolish son—that's how she referred to him, and I realized only too late that it was intended to hurt Sulo—she offered much advice in that regard. She mocked all the efforts we were making to get Gowthaman out of jail. 'Let's forget the past. From now on, we must try and protect what's still ours,' she said.

To keep Sulo company, the family barber's daughter and Sulo's mother's cousin stayed with her. Why was I living in that house as a person without an identity? It was puzzling even to me. Everyone became more and more anxious as the date for Sulochana's delivery drew closer. Since she knew the nature of her daughter's in-laws only too well, Sulo's mother gave me a substantial amount and asked me to take care of all expenses. I must have seemed like a saviour to her. We admitted Sulo in a reputed private nursing home two days before her delivery date. Yet the tractor operator's mother complained endlessly about the quality of service there. She thought it was because her son's mother in-law had no faith in her or her son that she had given me money and asked me to handle the expenses. Her hatred for me had ballooned as a result.

After the child was born, the old woman's brother visited the nursing home. Right from the start, he eyed me with suspicion. I had no idea what they discussed with each other but she was adamant that the child should be taken straight to their family home. When I overheard the two wondering whether the beautiful male child bore any likeness to their family, I was shocked. I sensed that a diabolical scheme was brewing in the old woman's mind, and became cautious. I decided that I should leave the nursing home at once. Though visibly perturbed, Sulo gave me her permission to do so. I handed over what remained of the amount her mother had given me. I also gave her the piece of paper on which I had written down the expenses incurred until then. She took it and, without even a cursory glance, kept it on the table. Just as I expected, her mother-in-law sprang forward and grabbed it. In front of everyone, she gave it to her brother and asked him to check the accounts.

'Best to check everything properly, just in case. We can't trust our own offspring these days. How can we trust an outsider? If we suspect something later, it will be awkward for the poor fellow,' she said. When I saw Sulo's lips quivering, I was pleased.

The old woman's brother scrutinized very carefully everything I had written. He raised many queries. When he grilled me repeatedly about the price of a bottle of medicine, I took the bottle from the shelf, gave it to him and asked him to verify the price. He was trying to compare the price printed on the label with the price I had listed. I was losing patience. I had to do something to protect my self-respect. His next question was nasty enough to push me in that direction.

'All right. I will present the accounts directly to them. Sulo, give me that sheet,' I said angrily and approached her. I had never addressed Sulo in the singular or by name in front of others. 'How dare you? Is she a woman from the barber caste? How dare you address her by name, and a familiar one at that?' her mother-in-law screamed. Unable to tolerate her words, I got ready to leave. Sulo was crying.

'This is why you should keep people like him in their place. Just to get by, a Nasuvan shaves in four houses and begs for food in eight. You let him into your house and allow him to move about freely, he will ask for this, that and the other.' She continued to provoke my anger.

Finally, reaching the end of my tether, I exploded. 'Did I come to your house with my barber's kit, offering anyone a shave?' I screamed, stomped out of the room and banged the door shut behind me. Two attendants and a nurse came running in alarm. Ignoring the elevator, I thudded down the stairs. When I reached the ground floor, Sulo's husband and mother-in-law were waiting for me. She was holding the bag in which I had packed my clothes. As soon as she saw me, she flung it in my face.

'Here is your bag. Why leave this filth behind?' she said, setting me aflame. Having lost all my self-control, I shouted out a harsh expletive at her. Then I started gathering my clothes which lay scattered on the floor. Taking me completely by surprise, the former tractor operator pounced on me from behind, and we began to exchange blows. Attendants from the nursing home along with a few timid doctors had started to form a circle around us. Both of us spewed torrents of abuse at each other. They had succeeded in destroying my dignity. It was then that I revealed in public the relationship I had once shared with Sulo. I had no recollection later of why I had done so or the words I had used then. But I am sure that I used extremely cruel words which they would never be able to forget. Unable to bear the insult, Sulo's husband collapsed into a chair in the hall. His mother began to scream at the top of her lungs. Then it was Sulo's loud wails coming from afar which helped me recover my wits. I couldn't say if it was really Sulo's voice or if I had only imagined it. But I came out of there instantly, leaving everything behind as if I had been chased away.

I thought someone was following me and calling out my name. Paying no heed, I walked briskly through narrow lanes reeking of sewage and reached a bus stop. I went to an all-night stall in the vicinity, sat on a greasy bench and ordered a cup of tea. Only when I looked for change in my pocket did I realize that I had left my purse behind in the nursing home. However, since I did have a few coins in my pocket, I managed to avoid being shamed by the stall owner. But I didn't even have the meagre amount I needed to travel back to my hometown. I started recalling some old friends who lived in that town. The house of a supervisor who had worked with me was close by, but I felt that it would be humiliating to seek help from him at that late hour. So I went in search of a childhood friend who worked as a labourer in a spinning mill. He lived in a bachelors' dormitory which was farther away. It was my bad luck that his room was locked. The guard looked at me with suspicion. Left with no option, I walked for half an hour and reached the bus station.

The station was teeming with passengers. Amid those countless people who had curled up on the cement benches or on the floor, resting their heads on bags and bundles, I found a place to sit and waited in anticipation of some miracle. I tried to think about what might have happened to Sulo. Whatever I could imagine was ghastly. I had taken revenge on her in the most cruel and unforgivable way. The old woman, too, would not forgive her easily. What if Sulo had, unable to bear the ignominy, come to a disastrous decision? I started sweating profusely. I was trembling within as I stood up and started walking. My feet moved involuntarily in the direction of the nursing home.

Standing on the deserted pavement opposite the nursing home, I looked up at the tall building. The ground floor, where the reception hall and dispensary were situated, was quiet. On the third floor, where Sulo was admitted, lights were on in nearly all the rooms. I tried for a long time to identify Sulo's room and check whether she could be seen moving about. My eyes were burning. I even wondered whether I should enter the nursing home on the pretext of retrieving my bag. I felt it would complicate the situation even further. I changed my mind. Since I couldn't think of anything else, I kept gazing at the windows on the third floor until sunrise. After standing on my feet for some time, I sat leaning against a lamp post. Within seconds, I fell asleep. At dawn, worried that someone might see me, I left. As soon as it was daylight, I met my childhood friend, borrowed some money and returned to the spot. I called the nursing home from a public telephone. I lied to the receptionist that I was Sulo's relative and asked to be connected. Once the connection came through, Sulo said, 'Hello?' I was listening to her in silence.

'Hello. Who is this?'

Relieved that she was still alive, I disconnected the call and walked towards the bus stop. A sudden, cold drizzle left me completely drenched. I boarded a bus to my village and took a seat. It began to rain heavily. When I reached home after an hour's journey, I was shocked to find that a side wall of our house had collapsed.

My sister started crying when she saw me. 'You didn't come home for three days. Where had you been, Anna? Yesterday, a snake crept into the house from god knows where. I was really scared. It was lying in the doorway for a long time. Then Ravi from the neighbouring farm turned up and beat it to death. After that, the rain started.'

The whole house was in a mess. Since the storm had dislodged a few tiles from the roof, a pool of water had collected in the veranda. I went looking for a carpenter. But I couldn't find him, and tried to do something on my own. After bailing out the water with my sister's help, I set out for the school.

I answered the headmaster's questions about Karunakaran's health and Gowthaman's appeal petition. Then I submitted an application requesting extension of my leave. From there, I went to the head office, met the district education officer in person and requested his help to process my application for a transfer. Then I returned home.

The next day, without my sister's knowledge, I went to her husband's house and mediated for a reconciliation. Using the sizeable amount that I had drawn as a loan from my provident fund, I redeemed her jewellery from the pawnbroker, took her with me to her husband's place and dropped her there.

After many years, I was all alone in the house. I spent four or five days thinking about moving on from everything that had happened and building a completely new life. At the end of the week, when I learnt that I had been transferred to the district office, I felt truly liberated. As soon as I joined duty, I decided to move house. I summoned my sister and sent all the household effects with her, barring a few items that I needed. Then I hired a flat in a multi-storeyed building at the heart of the district capital, and moved in with my meagre possessions and a few books. I stationed my old and damaged M-80, which looked like a museum exhibit, against the wall on the ground floor. Then I started making a conscious effort to free myself from both the fantasies of revenge that tormented me endlessly and my infatuation with Sulo. I tried gradually to read books, renew my old friendships one by one and immerse myself in work.

The relationship I had developed by chance with Sugandhi, a neighbour in the apartment complex, made my life in the congested town somewhat tolerable. Sugandhi's middle-aged husband made a living selling used clothes in the market. As happens in pornographic stories, two weeks after I moved into the flat, on our third meeting, I had sex with Sugandhi. I didn't even know her name at the time. A relationship that began when I happened to visit their flat for some reason continued for many months—until I met Sulo again.

I could sleep with Sugandhi whenever I wanted. For some months, I thought of her as a woman who was born to support me during a critical period in my life. I told her that too, whenever we fucked. She never asked me for anything; even so, I gave her money every now and then. Sari, ear stud, pressure cooker, underskirts, brassieres—I bought her things she liked and through them I was staking a claim on her body.

It was a relationship without the slightest complication. Sugandhi was adept at guarding our clandestine relationship. Whenever she saw me in public with a third person, she would move on as though she did not really know me. She was adventurous in bed. She unwrapped her whole body for me without any inhibition, and I was careful not to fall in love with her. I believed that there had never been any room for love in my life; or perhaps I resolved not to make room for it henceforth. I shared with Sugandhi only a few details about myself and my love affair with Sulo. She saw it as a typical love story, the kind popularized in Tamil films. She never said anything about Karunakaran or Sharada. I don't know what might have appealed to her in the story but she wanted me to talk about it again and again. She thought I liked talking about Sulo. She suspected that I was still in love with her.

'You never had sex with her?'

'No.'

'You didn't even kiss her?'

'We have kissed.'

'How many times?'

'Many times.'

'But you never did anything apart from that?'

'No.'

'Don't tell me you didn't even fondle her breasts?'

Such conversations happened between us only when we were having sex. I imagined that speaking about Sulo aroused her. Then, little by little, I began to reveal the hidden bits of my story. I didn't tell her how I kissed Sulo for the very first time in Karunakaran's office—it was *her* kiss, in fact—or how I forced open the pink-hued body of her love in the tent and filled it with my vengeance. I had considered these to be the most important and deeply intimate experiences of my life. But I realized only too late that Sugandhi was secretly trying to erase Sulo from my mind. She was convinced that her mature body could offer me greater satisfaction than Sulo's, which was slender like that of a little girl.

Sugandhi was also worried that I might abandon her and fall in love with a young woman like Sulo. Perhaps for that reason, or perhaps not, she kept expanding the scope of her engagement with me beyond sex. She washed my clothes regularly. At first, she used to cook and serve me my favourite meat dishes on Sundays; later, she started taking care of all my food-related needs. To forestall any suspicion on her husband's part, she took a certain amount from me for the food and gave it to her husband. She told me that her husband had accepted me as a paying guest. But I suspected that he knew the nature of my relationship with her.

Sugandhi yearned to go out with me. Giving in to her insistence, I once took her along to Palani, the popular pilgrimage centre. Registering under false names as husband and wife, we stayed at a lodge in the foothills for two days. We watched an old Tamil classic in a downmarket theatre in the town. Every time the heroine, who had devoted everything in her life to her husband, wept copious tears from unbearable sorrow, Sugandhi leaned on my shoulder and sobbed. The rest of the time, with her head on my lap, she kept stroking my penis. I caressed her breasts. We kissed ardently during the love scenes. Later, accompanied by lewd, titillating banter, we fucked all night. After bathing in the wee hours of the morning, we wore the new clothes we had bought the previous day and went to the temple. Everyone we happened to see—vendors of trays laden with votive offerings, women selling flowers, devotees—was shouting at the top of their voice. To avoid tiring ourselves out by walking through narrow pathways lined on both sides with shops, we rode the winch and reached the temple at the hilltop in no time. She bought two tickets for special worship: one for me and her, and the other for her husband, the vendor of used clothes.

All the while that I was with her, I watched out for any acquaintances who might appear out of the blue. She pretended that she had no such anxiety. Since it was a new-moon day, I imagined foolishly that Sulo might come there with her husband and child. I was also worried that I might run into one of my office colleagues. When we stood in the queue for a holy sighting of the deity, Sugandhi remembered to ask me my birth star. To the priest, she mentioned my name and then hers. I was staring at her transfixed as she paid obeisance to the radiant figure of Lord Murugan. It was then that I began to fall in love with her. This must also have been the moment when I began to think about continuing my relationship with her and making her mine. Two days later, for no particular reason, I abandoned such thoughts.

As far as possible, I avoided meeting or talking on the telephone with Sharada. The tragedies that had befallen Karunakaran and his family had quelled her yearning for revenge to some extent. She wanted to meet him in person at least once. She wanted to witness with her own vengeful eyes the full extent of his destruction. When she learnt that I had stopped going to their house, she seemed to realize that she might never have the chance to see him again. But I feared that she would make discreet inquiries about Karunakaran through other people and use my name to go to that house on her own some day. I became increasingly apprehensive about that possibility. Occasionally, my sister dropped in with her husband to see me. During those meetings, which were mostly confined to the office compound, we did not speak about anything specific. On one such occasion, my sister asked me a not-so-important question about Sulo. I did not reply. It was as if I had forgotten all about her.

Retaining Sugandhi in my life seemed to be the most important thing at the time. I was moving about freely in her apartment, almost like a family member. I spent at least two nights a week in her bedroom. In exchange for the help he received from me now and then, the vendor of used clothes had of his own volition surrendered his wife to me.

'Carry on talking,' he would tell us. He showed little or no hesitation in leaving us alone in the apartment. What kind of understanding was this? I was perplexed.

Sugandhi had begun to take liberties with me even in his presence. During the brief interval when he went to the bathroom, she would hug me tight, devour my lips in a flash and release them. At night, all three of us would lie down in a row. As soon as the lights were switched off, her husband would begin to snore. Without any hesitation, Sugandhi would come over and lie next to me. I imagined him listening to the sounds of our lovemaking. Like always, Sugandhi would take off all her clothes. She would also speak to me in quiet whispers. I feared that one day the vendor of used clothes was going to wake up suddenly and switch on the light, and this game was going to end in the most disgraceful manner. Not only did I anticipate such an end but, deep down, I wanted it too.

But nothing of the sort happened. The relationship and its intoxication continued without interruption. Some days, I would be overcome by guilt and disgust at myself. I used to think of Karunakaran as the embodiment of evil, and had wandered like a ghoul for thirty years wanting to wreak vengeance on him. Now I felt that I had become exactly like Karunakaran; in fact, in terms of morality, I had fallen far lower than him. But whenever I touched Sugandhi's warm body, which kept feeding me the wonderful and intoxicating fruits of lust, I was completely free of such feelings.

But Sulo intervened in my life again.

Nearly a year after I had last seen Sulo, I ran into Karunakaran's family barber. One night, when I was on my way home after buying a bottle of liquor for the night, he passed me near the clock tower from the opposite direction. When he saw me, he came running and held my hands.

'Haven't seen you in such a long time! How are you, Sir?'

Unable to bear the weight of the memories that suddenly began to crowd my mind, I led him to a hotel a short distance away. Even as we were walking, he started to tell me about Karunakaran. 'You left without a word. Was there any misunderstanding with Kavundar?' he said, standing at the hotel entrance and looking intently at me. After asking me where I was working, he inquired about my sister too. When I told him that she had gone back to her in-laws', he was happy. 'Such good news, Sir. Somehow the Lord Almighty seems to have opened His eyes.' Then he started telling me about Karunakaran again. 'He has become a pauper, Sir. He has given up on life. Once the life sentence for his son was confirmed, worrying about it knocked him off his feet. All his property and cash disappeared overnight. It's not clear whether he gave it all away to his lawyers or doctors. It seems he had a huge amount of debt to repay. Cars, jeeps, carts—he sold everything. Now he has nothing at all, Sir. Only a TVS-50, which is handy for running errands. Poor man, Sir. He won't last very long. They are counting the days. Can't you come by and see him once? Whatever you may hold against him, he had such affection for you. His kith and kin abandoned him. What else could they do? The murderer was our Kavundar's son. The victims were the children of their cousin. Who were they going to support—the killer or the victims? That's retribution for his past sins. Never mind, Sir. Pay them a visit.'

Speaking without a pause, he gulped down the coffee which had gone cold and started talking about Sulo. 'Only our Kavundar's daughter looks him up now and then. With an infant to take care of, she is also having a rough time. On top of that, I heard she works as a teacher in a school. She visits her father on weekends. Her mother-in-law won't allow her to do even that. Last week, there was a big row about it. "No one can stop me from seeing my father. If you want to keep me here, fine. If not, I'll go my own way," she said, removed her thali from her neck and threw it on the floor. Reporting all this to her mother, she broke down and wept. Who is to blame for this? I don't know whose curse it might be but it has destroyed the whole family,' the barber said with a sigh.

'Sulochana is working as a teacher? Are they so hard up for money?'

'It seems she can't bear to stay at home. Her mother-in-law is constantly finding fault with her, they say. Living with a woman like that is no easy task, Sir. With the sudden decline in their fortunes, they had no option. If the Kavundar's boy hadn't been convicted of murder, their situation wouldn't have been so bad. Using it as a pretext, their kith and kin got together and shut them out.'

From whatever he said, I tried to infer the name of the school where Sulo was employed. He did not know for certain. When he told me the name of the town where the school was located, though, I gasped in disbelief. Shaken and perturbed, I left quickly. After wandering aimlessly on the streets, I returned home shortly before midnight. Tiptoeing quietly up the stairs, I reached my apartment.

I had just opened the door when Sugandhi arrived. Rubbing her sleepy eyes, she called me for dinner. I told her that I had gone out for dinner with friends from my office; then I shut the door and drew the latch.

She made her displeasure evident the next morning. She would normally wake up well before me, prepare coffee and bring it to my door. But that day, she did not step out until eight. Opening the door once to send her husband away with his bundles of used clothes, she banged it shut immediately. I set out for office an hour earlier than usual. Hearing the squeak of hinges when I opened my door, she rushed out of her apartment and asked me in a husky voice to come inside. I entered her flat with a reluctance I had never felt before. After she had shut and latched the door behind us, she enfolded me in a tight embrace, breasts pressing against my chest, and began to cry. I was stunned. I extricated myself with difficulty and sat down on a chair. She perched herself on my lap and threw her arms around my neck. Tilting my head back to avoid inhaling the smell of green coriander that wafted from her mouth, I listened to her. Because I didn't speak to her properly and visit her apartment, she had not eaten a morsel last night. Pouting, she asked me whether I was angry with her. I made an inane reply. Then she insisted that I should eat something. 'I didn't even bring you coffee this morning,' she said and went to the kitchen. Feigning tension and anxiety, I lied that since I had to accompany the district education officer for an inspection, I had to leave right away. She was taken aback. 'All right. At least give me a kiss before you leave,' she said and leaned towards me. With a revulsion I had never felt before, I kissed her lips and got up. When I opened the door, she wailed, 'You will be back in the evening, won't you?'

'No. I'll be away for two or three days.' I gave her an off-the-cuff reply.

'Two or three days, is it?' she asked me in an odd tone and sighed. I ignored the question and stepped out.

The previous night, I had resolved to find out the name of the school where Sulo was employed and manage to meet her somehow. I caught an autorickshaw and went directly to the bus station. When Karunakaran's family barber had mentioned the name of the town in our conversation, I was astonished. It was the same town where Karunakaran had run his loan shop thirty years ago, and from where I had sent him a threatening letter two years ago to fashion an epic start to the saga of my revenge. Now I was reduced to this foolish mission of roaming around here in search of his daughter. I reckoned it was my third visit to the town in the past two or three years. The second time had been when Sharada had brought me here to remind me of her vengeance and my vow. Now, for some reason, the bus station was overflowing with people. I was bewildered. Only when I noticed farmers standing next to baskets loaded with vegetables and various types of fruits did I realize that the weekly market fair was on. It was good in a way: I would not stand out and risk being seen.

I had arrived at a time of day which was neither morning nor evening. If I had to meet Sulo, I would have to find out the name of her school and go there directly; or I would have to wait until the end of school hours and try to meet her at a bus stop or somewhere on the way. Though none of this seemed feasible, I had come here anyway. Since Sulo had not undergone any formal teacher training, I guessed she would be working in a private English-medium school and asked a few people whether they knew of such schools in that town. There were two high schools, one in the centre of town and the other on the outskirts. There was a nursery school as well. I went to the nursery school first, which was operating on the same plot of land as the tent cinema of thirty years ago where I used to sell murukkus for a living. Around twenty-five children were playing inside a small building with an asbestos roof. I told the watchman that I wanted to talk to the principal about an admission and obtained permission to go inside. Assisting the principal was a young teacher who must have been around eighteen. As she kept looking at me with an expression of dismay, I wondered whether she might know something about Sulo.

From there I went to the school in the centre of town. Since I was already acquainted with some of its office staff, I told them I was in town for some work and had dropped in casually to meet them. I sat in the staff room for some time, looking out for Sulo among the women teachers who walked in and out of there. All the teachers wore the same type of sari. Except for the principal, everyone seemed to be of the same age. If one watched them closely for some time, they might have even appeared to resemble one another.

Sulo was in a classroom, perhaps. If she happened to see me, a meeting might be possible. I asked the office attendant for directions to the bathroom. Then I sauntered past all the classrooms and came back. The classrooms were unbelievably quiet. I assumed that exams were underway. Suddenly, I was overcome by extreme revulsion at everything and left hurriedly.

Though I knew there was another famous English-medium school on the outskirts, I decided not to go there. I entered the bakery in front of the market fair, had a vadai and a cup of tea, lit a cigarette, and started watching the people who passed by. The town had changed totally in these two years—it was almost a small city now. I marvelled at the spectacle of its market fair. However, when I noticed the sharp-eyed loan sharks standing at the entrance, I was reassured that I had not come to the wrong place.

Then the memory of Karunakaran came to me.

He would position himself on the right side of this entrance—there was nothing like an entrance in those days—in front of the soda shop. Now there was a bangle shop in the same spot, and where Karunakaran had stood earlier, a thin young man was standing now. I thought the young man, who stood with his hands planted firmly on the seat of a parked moped, looking intently at everyone who passed that way, could be a loan shark. Exactly like Karunakaran, he had a notepad in his hand and kept turning its pages and checking the entries. Karunakaran used to keep his money in a pocket in his underwear. This young man carried a small handbag. Unlike Karunakaran, he looked harmless, even naive.

Karunakaran possessed a lean and hard physique. He must have been twenty-three or twenty-four at the time. Sporting a thick moustache twisted at both ends, he stood like a block of granite hewn for a sculpture. Those days I used to sell soda and bright-coloured drinks in the market fair. When the fair was on, Karunakaran would buy two bottles of soda from me every day. He never drank them, though. He would use the soda from one bottle to gargle and rinse his mouth, and the other to wash his face. He would stubbornly refuse to pay me. 'You call this soda? There's no gas in it. Did your boss give you water by mistake? I'll pay him myself. Go away,' was how he would end the discussion. I would be close to tears. Later in the evening, he would call me and pay up. Though I had grown used to it, I was scared each time that he might not pay.

He would nab those who were late with their repayments, yank them roughly like a predator dragging its prey, and station them at the entrance of the soda stall. He would create an invisible cage in the middle of that teeming crowd and shove them into it. 'Pay the principal along with interest first, then you may leave this spot,' he would admonish them, and then go on to attend to other tasks. He would violently attack anyone who tried to use this opportunity to escape. The abuses and expletives he used were disgusting and horrible, not fit for human ears. He had absolutely no respect for people who pleaded with him to be fair. 'We can't do any business if we are to play fair, Uncle. Keep your nose out of this. If he has a wife and daughters who are pretty and willing, he should bring them here, and then he can leave. Tell him that,' he would say, dismissing them bluntly. Even so, he continued to lend freely to everyone. When he arrived in town on the day after the market fair, he would be on his best behaviour. Like a kind and generous man, he would visit every street and lend money to all those who asked him for a loan.

Amma had borrowed a lot of money from him. Whenever he came to collect the repayments, he would enter the house and sit down. Older than me by a few years, my sister Sharada was studying in the ninth or tenth standard at the time. When he came by, Amma would send her away to a neighbour's house on some pretext. Yet his eyes did fall on her now and then. All kinds of things were going on in our house then. All kinds. I didn't have the opportunity to know everything, nor the ability to understand anything completely. In those days, I spent very little time in the house. My daily life was highly stressful.

Within a year of starting work at the tent-cinema canteen, my brain had turned into an alarm clock. Exactly forty-five seconds after hearing the final bell at twenty past four in the afternoon, I would reach the school's wrought-iron gate. I would cover the distance of half a mile between the school and my house in ten minutes flat, and arrive at home exactly at four thirty. Washing up took between five and seven minutes; then I spent between twenty-three and twenty-five minutes doing my homework. My younger sister, who was studying in the third or fourth standard, would arrive ten minutes before or after I finished my homework. When Appa entered the house, it was twenty past five on the timepiece in my brain. For about ten minutes, Appa would not say a word to anyone. He would spread a mat in the hall and lie down on it with his hands tucked under his head for seven or eight minutes. Then he would ask gently, 'Where has Amma gone?' Asking that question and receiving an answer from me or my younger sister would take him a minute. He would be quiet for thirty seconds. Then he would get up and go to the entrance, and stand there for three minutes, staring at the narrow alley opposite our house as though he was trying to catch sight of a mysterious person who was hiding there. Only after that would he order my sister to roll up the mat and lay it at the entrance. My sister would take two minutes to do it. After remaining patient for about a minute, Appa would scold her in a slightly angry voice: 'Useless donkey! I've been asking you to bring the mat and lay it at the entrance for one whole hour. What's taking you so long?' After my sister had brought the mat and spread it on the ground, Appa would look at me. I would shut my notebooks and shove them into my school bag, hurry inside and fetch the hurricane lamp that was last turned down at sunrise along with the kerosene bottle, and place them on the mat. My sister would bring a few scoops of ash from the mud stove. Then, sitting cross-legged on the mat, he would carefully remove the lamp's soot-covered glass chimney, put a pinch of ash on it and clean it with a rag even more carefully. My sister and I would stand two feet away and watch him, mildly anxious that the chimney might break. Cleaning the chimney and filling the lamp with kerosene took him ten minutes. He would then ask us to keep it in the veranda, get up, cover his bare chest with a towel and go out.

I would immediately start walking in the opposite direction and reach the canal in three minutes. I would sit among the palm fronds on the bank of the canal for four minutes to defecate. A pair of drongos would fly in and sit on the fence of twisted spurge. While shitting, I would watch idly as they hopped to and fro among the cactuses, shaking their tails which seemed to be split in two. By the time a garden lizard or sunbird or red-vented bulbul began to attract my attention, four minutes would be over according to the timepiece in my brain. Then I would get up in a flash. While washing myself in the canal, I would watch the shoal of carp leaping upward, sloshing about in the water, for thirty to forty-five seconds. Then I would tighten my loincloth, jump into the canal and swim between the banks, against and along the flow of water. When I lay on the bank, satiated with pleasure, the timepiece would scream that it was getting late. Then I would scamper up the bank, put on my shorts and rush home. I would reach home exactly at six. Sharada would have returned from her typewriting class. Sitting cross-legged on the mat, Appa would be either helping my younger sister with her lessons or harshly berating Amma. Or he would be taking in Amma's abuses through his wide-open ears while sitting in complete silence with his back against the wall. Or he would be drinking a cup of coffee without milk or reading that morning's newspaper that he had brought home from the library. Sharada would be busy in her cooking duties by way of helping Amma, or she would have gone to the public well to fetch water, or, standing in some secluded corner, she would be chatting with Dandapani from the blacksmith's house, who was an eleventh-standard student in our school. If I or anyone else happened to notice them, she would rush back nervously to the house and Dandapani would disappear quietly. Sometimes, Appa or Amma would admonish her severely. Whenever that happened, Sharada would stand leaning against the wall, with her hands folded behind her back, and shed silent tears.

Only once did I witness a version of this incident with the roles reversed. Amma and Sharada were in the kitchen. Sharada was screaming at the top of her voice. She was holding a stick of firewood aloft. Amma was kneeling in front of Sharada and pleading with her. She seemed to be pleading for forgiveness. Amma looked frightened. Tears brimmed over in Sharada's eyes. As her tears continued to flow, Sharada wiped them with her dhavani and kept on screaming. As soon as I entered, they fell silent. Appa arrived thirty seconds later. On seeing him, Sharada set down the stick of firewood, ran to him and sank into his chest. I watched in horror as Appa put his trembling arms around her, and Sharada wailed and cried like I had never seen before. Then Appa pushed her away urgently and turned to me. 'Aren't you getting late? It's a quarter past six already. Look, they've started playing records in the theatre,' he said.

Extricating myself from that environment, I listened intently and tried to identify the song. '*Inbamey, undhan paer penmaiyo?*' (Pleasure, is womanhood thy name?) It was a song from the film *Idayakkani*. The song was already past its second interlude. '*Panjanai vendumo?*' (Do you want a pillow?) was the line I heard. To be precise, it was the sixth song in the usual sequence of records. Immediately I checked the clock in my brain. It was eighteen minutes past the time I normally left for work. When I realized that neither the canteen owner nor his daughter Kantimathi would excuse this delay, I broke out in a sweat.

'Why are you so late, da?' Kantimathi would surely rap me on the head with her sharp-boned fist. The owner would laugh at me. The tea master would also feel like doing the same, but thinking perhaps that it would be disrespectful to burst out laughing in front of his employer, he would merely smile to himself. As soon as I imagined this scenario, I took off without even drinking the milkless coffee that Amma had prepared for me. Walking at a brisk pace, I reached the tent cinema sixteen minutes late.

Other boys had already stacked strings of murukkus and mixture packets on their trays and entered the tent. A few minutes had passed since they had started issuing tickets, and seven or eight men had collected in front of the canteen. The tea master was preparing tea. When she saw me, Kantimathi rushed over and, as if performing an important duty, rapped me on the head with her knuckles. Then she went straight to the cash counter and stood behind it. Rubbing my head, I made my way to the canteen, found my basket, sorted the strings of murukkus that were allotted to me and stacked them on a tray. Then I entered the tent carrying the tray and walked among the women who had begun to gather in the floor section, shouting, 'Mixture! Murukkei!' Thus, the day had started sixteen minutes late. Business, too, was terrible on that day. Most of the women did not buy any murukkus. During the intermission, I sold five teas and one bottle of coloured soda in the men's wing of the floor section.

Collecting a mere eighty paisa as commission for both shows combined, I headed home with a hungry stomach at two in the morning. There were no bondas or bajjis left over in the canteen that could be given to us. Since they had run out of milk during the intermission of the second show, I had finished washing the vessels an hour before the end of the show. Before going home, the tea master had asked with a laugh, 'So, you couldn't even get a cup of tea today?' But as I was leaving, Kantimathi gave me a few broken bits of murukku. I ate them as I walked home. I thought of the incident at home earlier that evening. Only then did I realize that it had been a day engulfed by misfortune. Most likely, it was on that day that my sister Sharada and I had gone to Karunakaran's loan shop.

On that unlucky day, Amma had ordered me to go to Karunakaran's loan shop and borrow a small amount. Since it was a holiday, I spent some time playing with tops with my friends in the open ground next to the Vellai Pillayar temple. I was already very late when I started walking towards Karunakaran's loan shop. On the way, I saw Sharada returning home from her friend's house. We ran into each other at the entrance of the market area. Thinking that I was loitering around, she asked me to come home with her. I lied that I had to meet my classmate Vincent to collect a notebook, and walked ahead. She started following me for no apparent reason. I was nonplussed because I could see no way of avoiding her. In the end, when I asked her to wait at the post-office gate and was about to go up the stairs to the loan shop, she joined me, again without any reason for doing so. I think Karunakaran had no inkling that Sharada would turn up there. Standing bare-chested outside his shop with a lit cigarette in his hand, he leered hungrily at the two of us as we climbed up the stairs.

Suddenly, I sensed that the young man standing at the entrance of the market fair was staring at me, and it made me anxious. To confirm that it was actually happening and was not a mere illusion, I started watching him. Sensing that my attention had turned to him, he shifted his gaze to the men who were entering the market. But he had also changed his stance so that he could watch me from the corner of his eye. To evade his attention, I entered the tea stall and sat on a wooden bench. Ordering another cup of tea, I took a samosa from a tray and bit into it. When I stood up to get a drink of water, I was taken aback to see the young man standing very close to me. Just as I had done, he ordered a cup of tea, then picked a samosa from the tray and had a bite. Then he sat down on the platform directly opposite the bench where I was seated, at an angle from which he could look me in the eye. I wanted to ignore him. To escape from my delusions, I picked up a sheet of the newspaper lying on the bench and hid my face behind it. I wondered if he could be one of my former friends from thirty years ago. But I had no reason to believe that of someone who seemed to be in his late twenties. So, I decided that it could be my imagination and tried to act normal.

Now the young man was staring at me without any inhibition. Every time I stood up—to return the teacup, to buy cigarettes or, later, to pay the owner—his eyes followed me. I also wondered whether he could be a relative of Karunakaran's, or an employee from his stone quarry or finance company. He could have seen me when I was staying in Karunakaran's house. He might even have guessed my identity but was perhaps too shy to ask me. At any rate, I expected him to approach me with a question. To give him that opportunity, I drew close to him. Now he seemed perturbed. Averting his eyes, he went out of the stall and reached the spot where he had been standing earlier. From there, he began to eye me stealthily again. Determined to free myself from needless speculations about him, I left quickly.

Since another three hours were left before the schools closed for the day, I wondered how I could pass the time until then. I thought of visiting the library. I went looking for the street with the library, which I had known intimately in my childhood. It was then that I noticed that the town had changed in every way. I couldn't recognize a single street. The newly risen buildings confused me. I was surprised that I had not noticed the change when I was last here with Sharada, and before that, when I had come here on my M-80 to post the threatening letter which Karunakaran never received, and which had disappeared without a trace. I doubted whether it was the same town that seemed to have lost not even an iota of its antiquity when I had come here with Sharada. Perhaps I had come to the wrong place? Fortunately, I was able to recall the name of the library and the street where it was located. I inquired at a provision store and a hairdressing salon, and then asked a cobbler for directions to that street. Just as I had anticipated, all three were certain that there was no street bearing that name. Later, still lost in a quandary, I arrived at the bus station. Intending to try my luck with a parrot astrologer who had taken up a small nook next to a wall with his birdcage and box of fortune cards, I put the same question to him.

The astrologer seemed to be in the throes of abject poverty. He looked at me as if at a strange animal—from head to toe, with a piercing gaze. Alarmed, I tried to get away from him. He stopped me and began to describe in detail the route to the street with the library. As soon as he started talking, memories of the place came back to me. I tried to cut in and tell him that I was quite familiar with the locality. But he seemed to be a man who would brook no interruption, someone who was overly keen to help others. He also seemed to have visualized that small town of his as a giant metropolis with a complex network of roads. I listened quietly to everything he said.

The area where the library was located was a patch of wasteland at the foot of a hillock. It was a barren plot surrounded by dense thickets of thorn trees and cactus, a site with which I was intimately familiar.

In our boyhood, we would bunk school and take cover in that fallow patch. My friends and I used to play marbles there. On holidays, we would catch garden lizards, piss on them to drive them crazy and then watch them. Some garden lizards turned truly insane. They would open their mouths and hiss at us. Sometimes one would even try to chase us. We would scream in fright. Then all of us would surround it with slender wunja sticks in our hands. In the end, there was no way out for the garden lizard but to die. Afterwards, by binding stalks of veldt grape with hill mango thorns, we would build a bier. We would decorate it with wildflowers, lay the garden lizard on it and carry it ceremoniously to the burial spot. Someone from our group would drum on his slate and play the frightening cadences of the bereaved. This procession would march until the far corner of the site. There, we would bury the garden lizard between thickets of prickly pear, then go and bathe in the small waterfall at the foot of the hillock, and return to our respective homes. No one was able to discover that wasteland of ours. Hiding in the clefts between rocks, we would secretly watch our parents and teachers wander all over the area, looking for us.

There were two or three jujube trees on that plot. We would pluck the fleshy, sweet fruits from the trees and offer them to our teachers. Students who brought jujube fruits for teachers were granted minor favours. We also supplied jamun to teachers to appease them. As far as I can recall, the jamun trees were also at the foot of the hillock. I remember that there used to be an old tamarind tree with thick branches beyond that patch. We would clamber up that tree like monkeys, sit on the branches with our legs dangling on either side as though we were riding horses, and chat among ourselves.

What else was there in that wasteland? I tried hard to remember.

I still have a clear memory of how, in the afternoon of that unlucky day, sitting on a branch of the tamarind tree, I had told my schoolmate Vincent about my vow of revenge. Amma had taken Sharada with her. I followed them for some distance. Then, after lying to them that I was going to meet the soda-stall owner, I took the shortcut to the Annanmar Sami temple. Once I reached the temple, I sat for a long time gazing at the idols of Ponnar-Shankar astride their horses, swords in hand, ready for war, fantasizing all the while that they would come to my aid, or offer consolation, or go to war with that loan shark for my sake.

There was no one at the temple. Round, unripe fruit lay scattered on the ground under the bilwa tree. An awful stench of blood was emanating from the dry carcasses of cockerels that had been impaled on the spears by someone seeking revenge on someone else. A small flock of mynahs had gathered on the branches of a towering Indian fig tree. I saw a blue-winged bee-eater sitting all alone on the broken compound wall. Bee-eaters looked like parrots from a distance. They had a thin body and a sharp beak like black drongos. I was aware that male bee-eaters had a pink ring around their neck like parrots. Someone had named them nasuvan kuruvis (barber drongos). Whenever I saw those birds, I used to wonder how they had got that name. Not even my Udayampalayam Periyamma, who was very fond of me and told us stories whenever she came visiting, knew why they were so named.

But I developed an intimate familiarity with those bee-eaters. Whenever I spotted them, I would stop and observe their movements. Watching them regularly over a long period of time, I learned a few things about them. That they had slender legs on which they hopped about, not staying in the same position even for a moment, was the first thing I noticed about them. I realized much later that they hopped about relentlessly only to escape the slingshots of amateur hunters. I was also the first to discover an incredible fact: being frightened and insecure always, the bee-eaters dug burrows in dirt mounds like rats and built their nests inside them. I told no one except Periyamma about this discovery, guarding it like a secret for a long time.

I committed a gross act of betrayal a few days later, when I happened to reveal what I knew about the bee-eaters to Thangavel, a boy from the house of soldiers who liked to hunt birds. Thangavel, who was a year older than me, was studying in a different class in our school. On a school holiday, we were loitering idly on the embankment of the canal. Thangavel carried a slingshot put together with thick belts. Rummaging in the debris of the broken wall in Achari's house, both of us filled our pockets with firm, round stones and set out on our hunt. Perhaps because he came from a family of soldiers, Thangavel was an expert in taking aim and striking the target. Unlike other boys, he was not at all eager to hunt garden lizards. He showed a keen interest in going after drongos, especially mynahs. Mynahs always liked to roam around in a flock. Totally reckless, they perched on tree branches, roofs and compound walls, shrieking relentlessly. Crouching in a spot they could not discover, Thangavel would fit a stone in the pouch of his slingshot, pull the rubber arms back and aim at the bird he wanted to hit. His eyes looked grim. An invisible shaft of light emerged from his eyes, extended in a straight line all the way to the small eyes of the bird and ended there. He inhaled deeply and held his breath. His chest expanded, nostrils flared and cheeks quivered. Everything happened simultaneously, each in consonance with the rest. The whole sequence took only a couple of seconds. He moved so swiftly that no one could make out when he had pulled the rubber arms back and released them. His hands went slack almost immediately and dropped to the sides. The same instant, I saw the bird lying under the tree. It lay inert and quite still, as though life had left its body a long time ago. Blood had gushed out from its eyes. Unaware of the death which had taken place without a sound and oblivious to the danger that lurked near them, the other birds continued to sit there. I wanted to run towards the tree to pick up the fallen bird but Thangavel signalled to me to stop, taking aim at another bird. Once, Thangavel had brought down three mynahs in this fashion, one after another. It scared me out of my wits.

At the canal one day, when Thangavel used his slingshot to kill a carp nibbling at the moss on the steps leading into the water, I became frightened of him. The supine body of the carp, lying inert and bleeding from the gills, kept appearing in my dreams for a long time.

I betrayed a couple of nasuvan kuruvis to him. It happened entirely by accident. One day, when he and I were walking along the canal bank, two bee-eaters were sitting next to each other on a low branch of a fig tree near the culvert bridge, hopping hither and thither. One of the birds held a pink-coloured insect in its beak. I had also discovered their burrow near a pile of displaced sand in the outer slope of the canal bank. Seeing us, the little birds became restless. As if by reflex action, Thangavel took out the slingshot from his pocket. By then, the birds had sensed danger and whizzed away.

Thangavel was despondent.

'Little sluts, they're trying to show me their tricks,' Thangavel cursed and ran down the slope after them. Since I knew the birds well, I stood still, watching him with a smirk on my face. Just as I expected, he came back a short while later looking crestfallen. He was gasping from the shock of humiliation. Full of hatred for the birds that had got away, he kept drawing the slingshot back and shooting stones in the air and into the water in the canal. He hawked and spat. I thought he might break down and cry. As if to console him, I said, 'Never mind. Let it go, the useless thing. It's only a small bird.' He tossed his head dismissively.

'We are not going to cook and eat it, are we? With this slingshot, I've even killed a vulture. You know that, of course. A small bird, that too a nasuvan kuruvi. Such a shame that I couldn't bring it down.' I was stung by his words. In no mood to talk further, I started walking home. He followed me. He had realized the reason for my anger. 'Ada. How could I forget that the bird was related to you?' He laughed and placed a hand on my shoulder.

I avoided meeting him for a whole week. One day, his father asked me in passing to come over to their house. I went there the next morning, feeling uneasy. Thangavel spoke to me as if nothing had happened between us. 'What's the matter, da? You haven't come by for five or six days. You two had a fight?' his mother asked. Then she brought two of his old shirts and a pair of shorts and gave them to me. Seeing the shirts, which were not all that worn, I was pleased and surprised. It was on our next holiday that I revealed to him the secrets I had uncovered about the movements of nasuvan kuruvis.

Dusk was falling and I was getting ready to set out for the canteen. Just then, Thangavel arrived with his slingshot. The pockets of his shorts were filled with stones. He wanted me to go with him to watch the nasuvan kuruvis. Instead of my regular frayed shirt sewn from tailoring scraps, I was wearing his old terylene shirt that still smelled of naphthalene balls. I had no other option but to accompany him. Thangavel marched ahead this time, leading the way. We walked in silence to the culvert bridge. With no help from me, Thangavel spotted the birds' burrow next to a pile of displaced sand. Going down the slope, he confirmed his discovery from the light green feathers scattered near the mouth of the burrow and came back feeling proud of himself. Then, as though he had planned it in advance, he dragged me to a hidden nook behind a thicket of milkweed plants. With a pounding heart, I squatted next to him.

Waving its brown arms, the sun was about to take its leave. Just as the thick, pink-edged petals of the milkweed flowers were about to close, the two birds flew in from somewhere and sat on a low branch of the fig tree. Seeing the insects they carried in their beaks, I thought that they might have stashed two or three nestlings in the burrow. 'Looks like they've hatched young ones,' Thangavel echoed my thoughts. Then one of them turned its body very cautiously and scanned the deserted embankment. The other flew for some distance over both banks, checked for the presence of anything suspicious or dangerous and returned to the branch. I pitied its foolishness in failing to detect us even while flying directly above the milkweed bush. Then they took off, one behind the other, from the fig tree, flew as far as the culvert bridge, and sat in the middle. They hopped slowly towards the edge and kept peeking at the burrow which was only two feet away.

Just then, the first record started playing in the tent cinema. '*Kodi malaigaliley kodukkum malia endha malai?*' (Of ten million sacred hills, which is the most generous?) The moment I heard the first line, I experienced a sudden stiffness in my body. When only the faint traces of the setting sun remained, the first bird entered the hole. Thangavel sat upright. Afraid that I might cry out, I clamped both hands on my mouth. The other bird sat on the rim of the opening and made a chirping sound. I couldn't tell whether there was any response from inside. The other one, too, entered the hole in a flash. There was complete silence for a few moments. Thangavel looked at me. I was about to get up. Just then, in a development that neither of us had foreseen, both birds came out of the burrow and, spreading their wings and holding them still, started wheeling in the air like vultures. Since it was getting late, I grew anxious. The timepiece in my brain started screaming. My head became heavy when I thought of Kantimathi. But within a couple of minutes, the two birds flew down and, as though they were on an urgent mission, rushed into the hole, one behind the other, and disappeared inside. Thangavel, who was crouching like a hunting dog behind the milkweed bush, drew himself upright and, without making a sound, reached the burrow in one leap. With the broken shard of a mud pot that he had kept handy, he tried to close the mouth of the hole. Alerted to the danger, one of the birds very daringly shot out of the opening, pushed through the gaps between his fingers, scaring him out of his wits, and flew away. The other bird was trapped inside the burrow along with the nestlings. The hole was quite deep. We probed the passage by inserting a stalk of elephant grass first, then followed up with a wunja twig. Since the passage curved after some distance, we couldn't get anywhere with these probes. Then Thangavel asked me to keep the mouth of the burrow closed and went away somewhere. Even as I was wondering what he might have planned, he came back carrying a mud pot filled with water from the canal. I could guess his intent and was appalled by it.

'I found it in the cattle shed of my grandmother's house,' he said, pointing to the mud pot. Then, cupping one hand like a funnel, he poured all the water from the pot into the hole. After we had poured five or six pots of water, the mother bird came out with drenched feathers, followed by four nestlings which had not even sprouted wings. Half dead by this time, the nestlings were crawling slowly towards the mouth of the burrow, dragging their pink-coloured bodies. The sight filled me with unbearable anguish. The captured bird did not survive even for five minutes. We couldn't tell, either, whether it was the father or the mother of the nestlings. We talked about it as we walked back. Not knowing what to do with the nestlings, we left them inside an empty vat of a molasses factory in the vicinity. When I rushed back to the canteen,

I was sweating profusely. I expected to be rapped on the head, but Kantimathi merely smiled when she saw me and disappeared inside.

At dawn the next day, I went to the molasses factory after collecting Thangavel on the way. The vat lay overturned. There was no trace of the nestlings. Over the next three days, we searched for them in all the surrounding bushes and stone piles. For more than a month following the incident, I had many melancholy dreams about the solitary bird which had got away. I don't know whether Thangavel had similar dreams.

A month later, on that day of misfortune, while I was on my way to Vincent's house, I wondered whether the solitary bird sitting very still on the broken compound wall of the Annanmar Sami temple was the one that had escaped from us. It was staring at me without the slightest hint of fear. I couldn't tell whether it was sorrow or vengeance that I saw in its tiny eyes. I left that place in a hurry, walked briskly along the shortcut and reached Vincent's house.

Vincent's father, known as Kuchi Police because he was thin as a stick, was at home. He must have returned from the police station only a few minutes earlier. When I entered the narrow hallway of their house, he was changing out of his uniform. He had removed his shoes. He had not yet taken off his starched khaki shirt or the hat adorned with red and violet bands. When he saw me, he called out to Vincent who was inside. Asking me to wait on the front pyol, he removed his hat and hung it on its usual peg on the wall. Then he took off his shirt. His ribs protruded against his filthy vest. Even as I was wondering how such a thin man could beat up prisoners, Vincent came out wearing a boys' lungi folded back up to the knees. He greeted me and led me out of the house. His father had begun to remove the khaki braces wrapped around his calves. As I watched him idly, I was puzzled, as always, that Vincent's father, with his dark complexion, could have such pale calves.

But why had I chosen to share an intimate sorrow of mine with Vincent? Brooding over it, I walked towards that patch of wasteland or the site that was reported to house a library now. Rejecting the path indicated by the parrot astrologer, I walked in the opposite direction. I was reluctant to go back to the main road and pass through the market fair. To avoid being spotted by that young loan shark's mysterious eyes, I walked through a maze of narrow streets crammed with houses. I wanted to walk along the foot trail that skirted the Annanmar temple and make a brief visit to the police housing colony. When I had gone looking for Vincent on that unfortunate day, I didn't have to walk this far. There weren't so many residences and so many narrow streets along the path I had taken that day.

That day, Vincent and I had reached the wasteland in no time. When I started talking about Sharada, Vincent stopped me and suggested that we should first sit on the branches of the tamarind tree as we normally did, and then we could begin our conversation. I thought it was a good idea. While growing up, I never trusted anyone more than Vincent. Like me and his father, the boy was thin. At school, both of us were on the list of good students. Both were keenly interested in sketching and drawing. Pathaiyampalayam Samuel Sir, our drawing teacher, loved us both equally. He also gave us equal marks.

On Sundays, we went together to the library. The librarian would never see either of us alone. He once made a remark about it to my father within our earshot. Most likely, the conversation happened in the library. Appa sat facing the librarian in an iron chair without armrests. The librarian was sitting in a chair that came with his position—one with armrests and a wire-knit seat. There was a wide desk between the two. Appa was sitting with his elbows on the desk. Vincent was showing me a page in a book of quotations from Periyar. I read a quotation from that page aloud but in a low voice. The words, printed in bold, black letters, went like this: 'There is no god. There is no god at all. He who propagates god is a scoundrel. He who worships god is a fool.' Vincent asked me in a low whisper whether I liked the quotation. I nodded. Then he asked me if we should write it on the compound wall of our school. Yes, I said.

Just then I heard my father laughing hard for some reason. When I turned to look, Vincent's father, the one who was nicknamed Kuchi Police, and Samuel Vadhyar were sitting on either side of my father, facing the librarian. Realizing that our teacher was in the room, we stood up and greeted him. Samuel Sir asked both of us to come closer. Reluctantly, we walked towards him and stood beside the three men. 'What is that book?' Samuel Sir took the book from my hand and glanced at it. 'Aha! So, you've started reading EVR's books this early?' he said with surprise and guffawed. Then he said, 'Why, our librarian feels bad that he can never see the two of you apart.' We were embarrassed. Gazing intently at us, the librarian said, 'But there is some secret behind it,' and chortled even louder than Samuel Vadhyar. Both of us were beginning to feel awkward. Then we came out of the room one by one.

Vincent was much more distraught than I was. We had learned to masturbate recently. Since we had been clueless about it until a few weeks ago, our classmate Swaminathan had taught us how to do it. Though older than us, he was our classmate now because he had been detained in the same class for two or three years. One day he had come over to our wasteland. Vincent and I were eating jujube fruits. Without warning, Swaminathan removed his shorts and showed us his erect penis. It seemed like a thing of wonder to us. Then he asked both of us to caress it. With a mix of diffidence, apprehension and intense curiosity, we started stroking it like he had shown us. He seemed like someone possessed by a mysterious force. Muttering something in a low voice about Pushpathal, a girl in our school, he closed his eyes. He was madly in love with Pushpathal. Though we didn't have any clear idea of love, we teased him about it all the time. Thinking about love and about Pushpathal, we started pulling hard at his prick. A few moments later, a brown-coloured sticky liquid spurted out of his organ. We watched in amazement. Afterwards, Vincent and I talked to each other in secret about it. The conversation continued over several days. It was during one of those days that both of us learnt to masturbate. I think the bond we had formed through that experience must have been the reason I had ventured to share a personal problem with him.

We sat facing each other on a sturdy branch of the tamarind tree. I began to narrate everything that had happened on that day as if it were a story. Sharada and I had gone to Karunakaran's loan shop. Karunakaran asked us to come inside and sit down. He gave us a snack and asked us to eat. Then he moved close to Sharada and touched her, and her body began to tremble. She tried to shake him off and escape from that room. He pushed me out with his rough hands, dragged her inside and shut the door.

I told Vincent everything. When I talked about blood trickling from Sharada's tender breasts, Vincent looked highly perturbed. After listening patiently to my story, he gave me a few ideas for wreaking vengeance on Karunakaran. 'If we had a gun, we could kill him easily,' he said, promising to smuggle his father's service revolver from their house somehow and give it to me. When I told him nervously that I didn't know how to handle a revolver, he reassured me that it was quite easy to learn. Since I didn't have anything more to say, I remained silent. He said he had to pee and climbed down from the tree. I too came down after some time. Vincent was nowhere to be found. For a few minutes, I waited for him at the foot of the tamarind tree. Then I tried calling out his name. 'Vincent! Vincent!' Since there was no answer, I walked around the plot looking for him. Then I saw him standing behind a bush, masturbating.

I had to part from Vincent within three months of that incident. I had not imagined then that I wouldn't be able to see him ever again.

Two weeks had passed since the school final exams had ended. Vincent was spending the summer vacation at his uncle's house in Kotagiri. He did not come back until the third week of May, when my family was suddenly forced to leave town. In fact, I had wanted to meet him on that last day. It was another day of misfortune when, for the second time, Karunakaran had pushed me out and bolted the door from inside. This had happened in the ancient-looking post office below his loan shop. Karunakaran's uncle had sent for my father that day. When Appa set out anxiously, thinking that Karunakaran would demand his money back, Amma went with him. Since I was sitting at home with nothing to do, I joined them.

Besides Karunakaran and his middle-aged uncle who were waiting for us at the post-office entrance, there was another person who looked like a ruffian. All three of us were stopped at the gate. On seeing Amma, Karunakaran took cover behind his uncle. Amma's face was flushed red with anger. Nostrils flaring, she glared at him and muttered something. Then his uncle said, 'Let's go inside and talk,' and led us into the post office, which was already open for business. Startled by our trespassing on the premises, the postmaster stood up hastily from his seat. Karunakaran's uncle pulled up a chair and sat down. All the blood had drained from Appa's face. Amma had begun to scream at everyone. I don't have a clear memory of what happened after that. But I do remember how Karunakaran, hiding behind his uncle, got very angry on hearing Amma's rant and came charging at her, how Appa blocked his path to stop him, and how Karunakaran's uncle caught hold of Appa's shirt, pulled him back and, in the most unexpected manner, slapped him hard on the face. Amma tried to hit back with another harsh invective. Then the situation spiralled totally out of control.

Understanding little of what was going on, I began to cry. I think my bawling must have been a nuisance for Karunakaran's uncle. He muttered something about it to Karunakaran. At once Karunakaran released Amma and came over to me. Grabbing me by my hair, he dragged me violently to the door, pushed me out and bolted it. As on the previous occasion, I stood outside the door in shock, not knowing what to do. I wondered whether there might be a sickle in the post office like the one I had found in his loan shop earlier, and looked around. I saw nothing except the desk, disfigured by countless smears of glue, and a few scraps of paper crumpled and tossed to the ground. Apart from these, there was a broken glass tumbler on the window sill.

From there, I went to Vincent's house. I must have wanted to call Kuchi Police for help. Since I knew that everyone in the house except Vincent's father was out of town, I couldn't have gone there for any other reason. But the house was locked. When I peeped through the keyhole, I found his hat hanging from a peg on the wall. At one end of the pyol, I could see his khaki uniform which had been taken off and flung in a careless manner. Even his leg braces lying in a messy pile. Then I went to see the librarian, and later, Samuel Vadhyar.

Luckily, there was no one else in the library when I got there. The librarian seemed to sense something from what I told him. He put on his sandals and set out with me immediately. Once he reached the door of the post office, which was bolted from inside, he stopped in hesitation. After aimlessly taking a few steps forward and back like a crow, he put his ear to the door. Then he took me by the hand and returned to the library. He poured some water from the steel flask on his desk into a tumbler and gave it to me. Then, assuming a teacher-like attitude, he advised me to go back home. When he saw me hesitating by the door, he pushed his chair back, stood up and came near me. As he put an arm around my shoulder and hugged me, he said in a low, gentle voice, 'They are discussing something. Nothing to worry about. Go on home.'

Having no other option, I left his office and went straight to Samuel Vadhyar's house. In the front yard, Samuel Vadhyar and a man I had never seen before were sitting opposite each other on folding chairs, engaged in conversation. On a stool placed between the two was a plate with a savoury snack, two stainless steel tumblers and a packet of Passing Show cigarettes. The other man held a small quantity of the snack in his palm. A cigarette was burning between Samuel Vadhyar's index and middle fingers. Bending his other three fingers inwards, he was holding a matchbox in his palm. On seeing me, he said, 'Come, da.' Perhaps thinking that I was loitering in that part of town on some pretext or without any reason, he asked, 'Are you feeling bored without Vincent?' and laughed. Then, paying me no further attention, he resumed his conversation with the other person. Later, as if he had suddenly realized something, he dropped the matchbox on the stool, stood up and led me outside the house, where he threw the cigarette on the ground and crushed it under his foot. Just as the librarian had done, he asked me in a low voice, 'Did your father send you here?' I remained silent, with my eyes fixed on the crushed but still burning cigarette butt near his feet. He asked me again, 'Did he ask you to get some money from me?' Even before that question, I had started crying. Perhaps because I had already recounted the incident to the librarian in a somewhat incoherent fashion, I was able to convey everything clearly to Samuel Vadhyar. Even as I was narrating the story, Samuel Vadhyar grew agitated. 'All right. I'll take care of it. You should go home,' he said. Then he went into the house, put on a shirt and came out with a small packet of the snack in his hand. He pressed the packet into my palm as though it were a secret gesture, then hopped on to a cycle that was propped against a wall and set out. From the direction in which his cycle was moving, I ascertained that he was headed to the post office; then I walked home.

Again, I had to cross that wasteland and the Annanmar temple, and walk along the deserted foot trail. As I was passing the temple, I heard a loud chirping sound from a low branch of a wunja tree. For some reason, I was alarmed. Bracing myself, I stopped and took a close look at the wunja tree, its branches sparse in summer. I could see nothing. Then, as I started walking, I heard the whoosh of something tearing through the air above my head. Looking up, I saw the bereaved nasuvan kuruvi and broke into a sweat. I picked up a wunja twig lying near the trail and kept swirling it over my head for protection as I walked.

When I reached home, Amma and Appa had still not returned. Sharada was applying henna on my sister's fingers. On seeing me, she asked casually, 'Where are they, da?' I gave her a vague reply. Without listening to me, she started saying something to my sister. 'Do you want henna too?' my sister asked me and turned away. When both sisters started giggling about something, I came out. There was a loud chirping sound from the opposite wall.

I had an inexplicable foreboding that we could not live in that house any more, that something might force us to leave town before the night was over. Appa and Amma, who would return home three hours later, must have been thinking seriously about it at that very moment. Most likely, they would not have discussed anything until they had crossed the Annanmar temple. Amma would have walked ahead of Appa. After passing the Annanmar temple, she would have waited for Appa under the shade of a tree. I couldn't say which of them would have been the first to start talking about vacating the house and leaving town. Appa would have tried to explain to Amma the problems involved in making a sudden move. Hearing Appa say that he was unlikely to get a transfer immediately, Amma would have been taken aback. 'Can't you take leave or something until then?' she would have asked Appa in the most pitiful manner. Either standing there or sitting on a small rock nearby, both would have started evaluating the possibility of vacating their house overnight, moving away to a different town and house, and raising the funds needed for the move. Amma would have told him about her thali which weighed two grams, and about the stud or anklet that was still in Sharada's possession. Appa would have been unable to say anything. Then both would have gone to the market fair to inquire about hiring a cart that would ferry them, along with their household goods.

Appa would have suggested that they should meet Samuel Vadhyar before leaving town. Vadhyar would have received them awkwardly and made them sit in the hall. Both would have drunk the coffee brought to them by Elizabeth Teacher. Teacher would have urged Amma to get Sharada married off soon. Then, with a mix of utmost reluctance and intolerable shame, Appa would have asked Samuel Vadhyar for a loan.

Samuel Vadhyar would have remained silent for some time; bending his fingers, he would have sat examining his fingernails without looking up at Appa's face. Or he would have exchanged glances with his wife, as if wondering how to respond. Then he would have reminded Appa of previous loans that he had yet to repay. Appa would have promised, without the slightest hesitation, that he would pay everything back on the first of the next month. Smiling faintly and looking at Amma from the corner of his eye, Samuel Vadhyar would have said as if he were speaking to someone else, 'The first keeps coming and going regularly every month,' and turned to look at Elizabeth Teacher's face. Amma would have tried to smile in embarrassment. Appa would have tried to get past that moment with a bitter sigh. Then Samuel Vadhyar would have given Appa a quarter of what he had asked for and urged him in a stern voice, 'Please give it back on the first without pleading for an extension.' It was that money which must have enabled them to hire a twin-bullock cart and bring it home with them.

I had begun to wonder whether there was anyone to whom I should say goodbye and whether there was anything to take away from this town. Vincent was the name I remembered immediately. It was horrible to realize that I might not have a chance to say goodbye to him. Apart from Vincent, I was somewhat close to Thangavel from the house of soldiers. Subramani from the Achari's house, Kodandasami who knew how to mimic parrots and squirrels, and Kantimathi who rapped me on the head—a few names came to mind. But on that fateful day, I could not meet any of them. In the end, I was able to say goodbye only to Soundararajan, who was playing a dice game on the platform of the Vellai Pillayar temple. We were not close at all, but when I told him that none of us would ever return to that town again, he appeared slightly shocked.

My sisters came to know about our impending move very late—well past midnight—when the twin-bullock cart that was to carry our household effects arrived and stood at the entrance of our house. Sharada was stunned. She wept, crying that she could never leave that town. Then Amma began to berate her for throwing tantrums. After all our household effects had been loaded on to the cart, Sharada went into the now-vacant house, searching for something. We had no idea what it could be. The rest of us had climbed into the cart and taken our places. Amma called out to her a few times, 'Sharada! Sharada!' Then she got down from the cart, seething with anger, and entered the house. Appa had lit a cigarette. I was thinking about the pink-bodied nestlings which had gone missing. As if oblivious to everything around her, my younger sister sat clutching her school bag. Her eyes were heavy with sleep.

Suddenly, I realized that I was standing on one end of the street with the library that the astrologer had mentioned. In fact, I had not passed the wasteland or the Annanmar temple which were on the way to the library. I wondered how I had managed to get there. Because I had been preoccupied with useless, irrelevant thoughts, I might have failed to notice them. From the spanking new signage on the street corner, I tried to ascertain if it was indeed the street I was looking for.

It was the same street of thirty years ago only because its name was unchanged. All the other identifying markers had undergone a sea change, and the street seemed completely unfamiliar to me. Of the houses that stood on the street thirty years ago, I couldn't find even one. As if according to a plan that someone had drawn up, all the earlier buildings had been removed and newly designed houses placed in orderly rows in their stead. On a street that was once filled with neem trees, portia trees and shrubbery, I found only a few crotons and saplings of asoka trees. In the absence of any garbage, debris, dust and the like, the street appeared neat and orderly, as though it was not yet open for use by the public.

There was no human presence as far as the eye could see. Descending vertically from the midday sun, the heat dashed against the buildings and scattered in all directions. It was draining my blood as if in cosmic retribution. Though exhausted in body and spirit, I walked on. I was sure that the library was no longer housed in the old building. Since I was not sure where the library might be on that street which stretched into the horizon in a straight line, I looked closely at every building. I believed that there would at least be a signboard to identify it. It was not merely a belief but a logical inference, for there were signboards in front of every building. Most of them displayed the name of a man or a woman and the post they held. On signboards installed for what appeared to be offices, the names of the buildings were written in bold letters. I presumed that the library too would be housed in a huge building and a signboard would certainly be installed at its entrance. However, until I reached the end of that street which stretched over an incredibly long distance, I did not see any such building or signboard. I must have, in fact, walked much farther than I imagined.

I was totally exhausted when, by a stroke of luck, the street came to an end. However, there was a huge wall blocking my way, preventing me from going further. It felt as though I was trapped in a prison cell. I scoured the wall hoping to find a way to escape—like a small door or a hole. When I realized that the wall had been designed carefully to ensure that no one could escape, I was utterly dejected. At a loss, I stood with my back against the wall and tried to think. I couldn't find even a small patch of shade where I could protect myself from the scalding heat and blinding light. Even if I wanted to get out, I would have to go back the same way that I had got here. With all its fluids having dried up, my body was close to evaporating. I doubted that I could cover such a long distance with a body that was drained of all its energy and turning into a corpse. I also suspected that, on the way back, the distance might simply double itself. I cursed myself for naively trusting the words of a parrot astrologer and going on a foolish misadventure only to find myself stranded without hope. Someone had to come here now to rescue me and take me back to my former world. Some unrelated person. But it didn't seem like a fantasy to me. Feeling confident that he would arrive shortly, I lit a cigarette.

Just then, at the far end of the street, at exactly the spot where I had stepped into this mysterious zone, the shape of that person appeared like a large beetle. Or did it resemble the dragonfly that I trapped in a matchbox and played with as a child? I could even hear the droning buzz of its wings. It was doubtless the person I was waiting for. I started to feel tense. My heart was racing. But the person was none other than the young man who had stood at the entrance of the market fair like Karunakaran and kept a close watch over me. I decided to deal with him firmly this time. Like a rescue vehicle sent in response to a distress call, his TVS-50 arrived with a roar and stopped near me. Planting his right foot on the ground, the young man asked me—without any sense of tact, as though he was privy to my personal life—an impudent question. 'What's up, Sir? Are you looking for the library?'

I felt humiliated. I wanted to retaliate right away. 'No. I didn't come here looking for the library. I am heading to the post office,' I said in a neutral voice, as though I was talking to a stranger, and kept walking.

'To the post office, eh?' he said as he opened the throttle gently and brought the vehicle closer to me. Feeling perturbed, I tried to move away.

'Yes, they told me that it was here somewhere.'

'Did they really say that?' He sounded surprised. Then he looked at me with a pensive expression on his face. 'All right. Sit behind me. I'll drop you,' he said and revved up the engine. Without betraying my sense of defeat and humiliation, I sat on the pillion. The smell of sweat that came from the young man's body reminded me of Vincent. I wondered whether he might have some connection with Vincent and was about to ask him when I noticed, to my surprise, that his vehicle was travelling along the foot trail adjoining the wall of the Annanmar temple. Even more important, he had passed the school where we had studied thirty years ago and was now going past the wasteland which was once the site of our secret exploits. As we passed the tamarind tree with its thick branches on which Vincent and I had once sat facing each other, I slipped and tumbled headlong into the past. Feeling like the same boy who had stood defiantly before Karunakaran and sworn revenge while holding aloft a blunt sickle that was too heavy for him, I was about to jump off the vehicle. At that precise moment, the young man steered his moped close to a spanking new building. When I saw the brand new signboard of the post office displayed at its entrance, I was even more desperate to jump off and get away from him, like a wounded bird with broken wings. As though he had anticipated such a move on my part, he brought the vehicle to a dead stop.

'Sir...'

I had no other option. Besides, I didn't want to seem like an ingrate. He looked as though he was eager but reluctant somehow to ask me about something. He placed the vehicle on its stand, came over to me and asked me in a hushed tone, 'Is your name Karunakaran?'

I was so taken aback that I couldn't reply.

After scrambling up my sense of time, he disappeared. I was astounded by the size of the building which appeared totally incongruous in that small town. Trying to believe that a dilapidated granite building and the ruins of Karunakaran's abandoned pawn shop on its first floor had never existed on that site, I entered the post office building with extreme diffidence. Inching forward like a legless reptile across its marble floor, I looked for—among the four or five employees of both genders who were visible through the windows beyond the glass partitions—that elderly postmaster. On the other side of a small opening in the glass partition sat a young woman who looked like she had been expecting me to show up. She looked up at me and smiled as if in greeting.

'How may I help you, Sir?'

I wanted to ask her about the elderly postmaster who looked like the very familiar and restless ghost of my father. However, unable to muster the courage, I extended a ten-rupee note instead, as I had done the last time and the time before that, and said in the same hushed tone, 'One inland letter, please.' Just as I had expected, she opened the drawer of her table to check and, pouting, said, 'Sorry, we are out of change.' I was ready for this. Suppressing the laughter that came bubbling up from within, I requested her to give me postage stamps for the balance amount. As though she had kept everything ready, she held out the inland letter and postage stamps in no time. While receiving them, I caressed her fingers deliberately. She flashed me a pretty smile.

'Thank you.'

'Welcome.'

But as if our transaction would be incomplete without another brief sentence, I stayed put at the counter. Pretending not to notice me, she looked down and got busy with something else. Then she looked up suddenly, as though she had just remembered that sentence. Pointing with her left hand, pink bangles tinkling, she said in a gentle voice, with a hint of apology, 'The glue is on the window sill.'

Then I stepped outside.

The young man was waiting at a roadside stall on the other side, with the snare of his covetous gaze fixed on the entrance of the post office. My hands shook. My whole body must have been trembling too. Filled with loathing and anger, I tried to walk past him. Hastily flicking away the cigarette that was burning between his fingers, he followed me anxiously. Increasing my pace gradually and covertly, I tried to break into a run. He chased me. I gasped for breath. Then I smelled the familiar odour of his sweat and, having no other option, braced myself and stood still. I turned around and tried to meet him face to face. He was panting too, and sweat was pouring from him. As though he was unable to string words together, he asked me in a halting, shattered voice, 'Sir, you are not Karunakaran, then?'

I was ready with the answer. 'No. I am certainly not Karunakaran.'

He stumbled. 'Then … who are you?'

I sighed. 'Someone else.'

Very soon I had transformed into a different man, a person empty of vengeance, love, or anything else that was real and concrete. Even the relationship between Sugandhi and me had changed completely. I could not tell if it had changed on its own or if I had changed it deliberately. I had visualized her as my wine glass or as an ice cube floating in it. I hated both these metaphors of intoxication. I could not make out what she might have pictured me as. I clung to her as to an unavoidable evil and an incurable addiction. We fought often and abused each other with cruel words. Our neighbours and her husband, the vendor of used clothes, watched our quarrels without attempting to intervene. On some days, I would loudly declare within everyone's hearing that I no longer had any relationship with her, go into my apartment and slam the door. On other days, she would be the one to do it. But it was very likely that we would be sleeping together that same night in the same bed, either in her apartment or mine.

Before long, her husband had turned into a former vendor of used clothes. I had set up a small 'cut-piece' store for him. When her husband knocked at ten in the night,

Sugandhi would walk nonchalantly to the door, rearranging her dishevelled clothes, and open it for him. As though he was trying not to look at her face bruised by my kisses, he would slink into the kitchen with his head down. Later, he would tiptoe like a thief to the tiny hall in that apartment and lie down on a folding cot, covering himself from head to toe with a blanket. Within the next few seconds, the sound of his snores would turn into smoke, sneak into our bedroom, bolted from inside, through the gaps in the door and hide under our bed like his loyal spy.

I firmly believed that his snoring was fake.

Whenever he saw me alone, he tried to smile. As if paralysed, his eyeballs would stay transfixed on me. As though his heart was filled with hatred for me and he should never allow it to spill out until the moment was right, his behaviour would betray an abnormal sense of caution. I thought he might have vowed to take revenge on me for snatching Sugandhi away from him to fill my cup of emptiness. I thought of him as an animal on the prowl, waiting for the right moment to fulfil his vow. Some nights, when Sugandhi and I were together, he would barge into the room on purpose, asking for a blanket or a towel. Feeling flustered, I would try to move apart. Sugandhi would get up calmly and give him what he asked for, or she would simply lie there and let him take whatever he needed. Sneaking furtive glances at her nakedness, he would leave the room. At such moments, I wondered whether he carried a hidden knife or sickle on his person. That former vendor of used clothes might also have set a deadline for fulfilling his vow. Unbeknownst to Sugandhi, I was trying to watch his movements and uncover his secret plans. My hands had begun to tremble while opening the envelopes of personal letters I received at home or in the office.

However, like a student who tries to leap on to a moving bus or like a trapeze artist, I had begun to crave risky adventures. I tried to transcend my destiny in a topsy-turvy and ridiculous manner. Demeaning my friends' ideologies and hopes with brutal remarks, I tried to disrupt their equanimity. Even the few friends I had left were moving away from me.

One day, after looking high and low for Sulo, I had returned home well after midnight. As soon as I entered the apartment, as if by involuntary reflex, I looked at myself in the mirror. It was an unimaginably horrendous experience. I wondered whether there was something wrong with the mirror or my vision. I suspected that I might have lost my mind. A very old black-and-white image of Karunakaran from thirty years ago appeared before me on the surface of the mirror, like an old photograph inside a picture frame. I tried to touch it with my trembling fingers. I kept trying to recall the face of the parrot astrologer who had guided me, the face of the young loan shark who had followed me, and the face of the young woman in the post office in the seat formerly occupied by the elderly postmaster—a dead ringer for the implacable ghost of my father—who had allowed me to caress her fingers. Only then did I begin to suspect that I might have imagined all of them. I wondered whether I had gone there at all. Was I standing bewildered in front of the mirror right after waking up from a nightmare, still believing that it was all real? Then I remembered to check my trouser and shirt pockets. In my shirt pocket I found two or three crumpled, pink-coloured bus tickets. But I couldn't find the envelope with the stamps in it that had been folded double and secured in my shirt pocket, the envelope I had received in exchange for a ten-rupee note from the young woman who had greeted me from behind the glass counter in the post office that was functioning in a brand new building erected in the wasteland of our childhood. An inland letter, and stamps for the balance amount. In that case, it was certainly a dream or a hazy memory of an incident that happened a long time ago. Was I standing before this small mirror with its faded silvering, which I had been using for a very long time for shaving and combing my hair, unable to free myself completely from the harsh grip of a severely muddled sense of time?

I might have bought these pink-coloured tickets during a journey on some other day and put them in my pocket. It seemed somewhat logical. To get rid of the vestiges of that nightmare and to shake off my drowsiness, I went to the bathroom. When I looked up after washing my face, I was shocked to see an inland letter, folded in four, lying in the small niche for the soap. I picked it up with trembling fingers and tried to open it. From that envelope folded in four, postage stamps spilled out. My whole body had begun to quake and tremble. By the time I bent down and collected the scattered postage stamps, I had begun to lose consciousness. The postage stamps were adrift in a small puddle that had gathered on the rough cement floor of the bathroom, like little paper boats that children set afloat in streams of rainwater. While I was trying strenuously to collect those tiny bits of paper, I heard Sugandhi's voice.

It was most likely at that moment that I decided to completely sever my relationship with the past.

A misunderstanding had developed between Sharada and me as well. I had also fought with my younger sister's husband over a trivial matter. Since I was no longer trailed by anyone's shadow, I was moving about freely with Sugandhi. When people ran into us in movie theatres, parks or hotels, I introduced her to them without any inhibition. Sugandhi had changed herself completely. She was no longer the pathetic girl who got married to a vendor of used clothes by accident. She was the pretty young wife of the owner of a cut-piece store. Her skin had grown softer. She had begun to wear fine clothes. The elegance and appeal of her deportment kept growing. She had even learnt to use a few English words while speaking to some of my friends. I was baffled, unable to figure out where she had picked up such verve and style. In the company of other men, she had begun to act coy and, biting softly into her lower lip, she would draw the free end of her sari delicately over her breasts. When she attempted to cover her breasts even in front of the vendor of used clothes who happened to be her husband, I wondered whether it might be a sham.

Later, I asked her about it too.

'Now I don't feel desire for anyone except you,' she said. 'I don't let him anywhere near me. But he keeps pestering me. We end up fighting every night.' I didn't know whether to believe her or not. But, little by little, I had begun to fall in love with her. Even though my ardour for her body was waning, I thought of taking her as my wife. She was only too willing to leave that former vendor of used clothes and come away with me. Every day we would contemplate the best way to broach the matter with him. I started asking a few of my friends for advice and suggestions. Whenever my friends from the office happened to see her, I saw the flames of jealousy burning bright in their eyes. Innumerable canards about me had begun to circulate in the office. I thought one or two of my friends had begun to develop a kind of craving for Sugandhi's body. Sugandhi complained to me about one of them who visited my apartment in my absence and used the opportunity to chat her up.

'He keeps staring at me and his eyes stray all over the place. Even the way he speaks to me is inappropriate. He uses double entendres all the time.' She sounded really scared as she said all this to me.

Two days later, I met the man in a bar and gave him a piece of my mind. He was rattled. The canards that had already been circulating about me began to multiply at an incredible rate. On the wall of one of the latrines meant for outsiders on our office compound, someone had drawn a caricature of me with a big penis, the office cleaner reported. Wanting to see it myself, I was about to get up from my chair immediately.

'I erased it right away, Sir,' he said and warned me to be careful. After that, I started introducing Sugandhi boldly as my wife. I considered introducing her to my sisters and a few relatives. I especially wanted her to meet Sulo. Sugandhi wanted that too.

Her husband looked as though he had aged suddenly. In one year, more than half the hair on his head had fallen out. Doctors were increasing the power of his glasses once every six months. Like a stage actor, he had chosen a thick black frame for his spectacles. When he stared at others from behind those glasses with suspicion and fear, the enlarged image of his motionless eyes looked menacing.

He coughed relentlessly at night.

Being forced to listen to his endless coughing spells in that apartment was unbearable. I wondered whether he was doing it deliberately to annoy us. One day he began to cough violently. Sugandhi and I were in the only bedroom in that apartment, with the door bolted from inside. He was lying on a folding cot in the hall. When I had come into the apartment half an hour earlier, his eyes were closed. I had entered the bedroom without disturbing him. Sugandhi, who came in with her hands wet from doing chores in the kitchen, bolted the door from inside and came to me. I was very tense. She had refused to have an abortion this time. 'I want your baby,' she whispered in my ear as she leaned on my chest. Not knowing what to say, I grabbed her breasts. She freed herself and sat up. 'Why are you thinking about this all the time? Here I am telling you something, and you seem to be thinking of something else,' she said angrily as she lay her head on my lap, lifted my hands and placed them on her breasts. 'This is meant only for you and nobody else,' she cooed.

I tried to appease her. I told her that we would abort the foetus just this once, then we would get married quickly and have as many children as she wished. What I told her sounded far-fetched even to me. She burst into tears. She must have realized that not one word I said to her was true. Thinking that I could cheer her up with a kiss, I had begun to savour the astringent taste of her lips. It felt as though an incident from long ago was playing out again. I thought I was repeating the sentences I had spoken long ago to someone else.

It was then that her husband started his horrible coughing fit. At first, both of us ignored it. But hearing him cough made her anxious. Freeing her lips from mine, she tilted her head to one side, like a rabbit, and listened carefully to the sound. Until his coughing ceased, she lay still and stared at the bolted door. Getting up without a sound, she stood with her eyes glued to the gap in the door. Then she came back and whispered, 'He is fast asleep,' and leaned on me.

When our lovemaking was beginning to get intense, he started coughing again. This time, I became more perturbed than her. Like a clock hand turning at high speed, I swivelled my neck in the opposite direction and kept staring at the closed door. With her feeble arms, she tried to turn my perspiring face towards her. 'That's nothing. Come here.' She moaned as she embraced me and tried to press my face on her erect nipples. But when his coughing became more intense than ever, her body began to grow limp. We heard phlegm rattling in his throat. She became distraught. She leapt from the bed as though she had sensed a calamity, and even as she was clasping the hooks on her blouse, she ran to the door and opened it. I followed her.

Her husband had fallen from the cot. His body was soaked. An unbearable stench assaulted my nostrils. Acting quickly, I tried to lift him and lay him on the cot. Muttering something in a low voice, Sugandhi came to help me. His body had grown stiff. Saliva dribbled from his mouth with a rank smell and trickled down his neck. 'Aiyo! What's happened to him? Muruga!' she cried, wiping his face with the free end of her sari, and hurried to the kitchen. I turned up the speed of the electric fan to increase the air flow and stood perplexed, not knowing what else I could do. After splashing water on his face, she tried to rub his numb soles to warm them. While we were wondering whether to take him to a nursing home or call an ambulance, he opened his eyes. She thanked some god and held him against her breasts while asking him anxiously, 'What happened? What happened to you?' Wanting to do something about the situation, I went immediately to a nearby clinic and brought a doctor home. Within the next one hour, her husband sat up and looked at us. His face had cleared up. He appeared to have derived some kind of consolation from what had happened there that evening.

Worried, but also relieved that nothing serious had come to pass, Sugandhi stood before her husband with her hands folded across her chest like a servant. He looked at her first, and then at me. Lacking the courage to meet his gaze directly, I lowered my eyes. But his gaze, which loomed over me like a solid object, made me gasp. I stood transfixed like a trapped animal. My eyes, which were focused on a patch of the floor of about two square feet, did not register anything else after that. I realized that this could happen again in the future—in some other environment, to someone else. I imagined that then, too, I would be standing as a witness to the incident as I was doing now. As witness or cause, I couldn't say. The prospect, imaginary for now, was terrifying. Slithering like a rat snake, I crept out of there quickly, entered my room and bolted the door.

In truth, I had no plan in mind at that moment. But within just a few minutes, I came to a firm conclusion that I had to go away, severing all contact with Sugandhi and that former vendor of used clothes. I was ready to leave. Fantasizing about my life in the future and a world in which no such incident could occur again, I gathered my clothes and stuffed them into a Rexine bag that was in a reasonably good condition. I picked up the jeans that lay crumpled on the chair, pulled them on and dashed out. When I realized that I had not taken my wallet, I kept the bag near the door and went inside. Unable to find it in any of the usual places in the apartment, I figured it must be in Sugandhi's bedroom. But I decided against going there to retrieve it. As had happened many times before, I was prepared once again to spend another night without a paisa on me. I stepped out. As expected, Sugandhi was waiting near the door. She had placed a hand on the doorknob and was about to push it open. Paying her no heed, I rushed past her and started running down the stairs. Accompanied by the loud clatter of her anxiety, she followed me.

'Aiyo, what's wrong with you? Where are you going at this unearthly hour?' she cried and tried to grab my shoulder. 'Are you angry with me? I am truly sorry. What else can I say?' Wailing, she ran ahead of me and tried to block my way. 'What do you mean by leaving without a word in this situation? I won't let you go,' she screamed and tried to snatch the bag from me. I grappled with her. Noticing that our neighbours were watching us, she lowered her voice. 'All right. At least tell me where you are going. When will you come back? If you don't come back, I will kill myself!' she muttered in a subdued and menacing voice. Alarmed by her threat, I stopped for just a second. Then, without another word, I disappeared from there.

Without a single rupee in my pocket, I walked around aimlessly for hours. Instead of brooding over this severance that Sugandhi would never be able to forgive, I began to reflect on my solitude. I thought of myself as someone who had been forsaken and betrayed by everyone. Tears welled up in my eyes. The town was in one of its savage moods. Vehicles were frantically racing past one another. Like a pathetic vendor of used clothes who is despondent about having to go home without having sold anything, I kept wandering through the back alleys of the town, a bag full of clothes slung over my shoulder. Once I reached a prominent thoroughfare, I stopped at a random bus stop that appeared to be deserted. At least the vendor of used clothes had other things in his life. A small apartment. A compact bedroom. A narrow hall. A folding cot. A beautiful, young wife with big breasts. His wife might be having an affair with some other man. And that other man might have seized his bedroom and cot along with his wife. But it was not a problem at all. If the husband coughed violently once, ribs aching and eyes nearly popping from their sockets, it was enough to restore everything to him. There was no chance of his becoming a nobody overnight like me—a man who had nothing, who wasn't anybody, who was not a vendor of used clothes, or a loan shark, or a guileless and foolish husband, the kind that Sulo and Sharada had been destined to marry. I was moving about without shape or direction, like some useless liquid spilled on a smooth floor. This was happening over and over again. Again and again, I found myself stranded in a similar place at a similar hour, a pauper like I was now, thinking about something pointless like this. My sole possession now was this bundle of old clothes in a Rexine bag, and the place where I had ended up was an anonymous bus stop. The only thing I could think about now were the big breasts of some woman who had got married by chance to a vendor of used clothes and the astringent kisses from her dark red lips that looked like strips of red meat.

To free myself from these revolting thoughts, I started thinking about something else. About something else meant ... about Sulo. It was true, though it was humiliating to admit it to myself. Instead of Sugandhi's big breasts, I tried to think about Sulo's small ones, which looked like two upturned chrysanthemums. But since this metaphor could also remind me of Sharada, I strove anxiously to abandon the thought. Whenever I thought about Sulo, I couldn't avoid thinking about Karunakaran too, and then about my vow of revenge. Then I would have to travel once again towards my past—that is, travel backwards in time over a period of thirty years. And I imagined that I had left all that behind.

Before long, I had begun to think about the wonderful fragrance of royal jasmine that belonged only to Sulo. Just then, as though something that had transpired already was happening again, Sulo arrived with her baby at the bus stop where I was waiting. She smiled at me as if nothing had ever happened between us before that moment.

~

THIS STORY ENDED QUITE SOON afterwards—very soon, in fact. Sulo had appeared before me like a ghost who put an end to everything: my vengeance, which could never be wreaked; my vow, which could never be fulfilled; my love, which had turned bloodless and pale; my lust, without form, taste or colour, which had dwindled to nothing. I couldn't tell whether she was a benign or evil spirit. In truth, when she smiled at me, I didn't recognize her at all. I couldn't believe how much she had changed. The woman before me was not the cheeky young girl I had met for the first time, nor the pitiful naïf in the nursing home wilting under the burdens imposed on her. That she looked slightly filled out now was not a drastic change. But an unpleasant and frightening shift was evident in her narrow eyes. A stench that could not have been hers wafted from her body. She was not perturbed at all on seeing me. Even when she spoke about Karunakaran, no profound grief was discernible in her voice. Her demeanour was friendly and courteous. 'Why don't you come home sometime?' It was her formal invitation to an acquaintance she was meeting after a long time. Given my situation, I had no option but to accept what could hardly be considered an invitation. Nonetheless, that was how it seemed to me at the time. I left with her immediately. She had sensed that I had no money with me. She boarded the bus through the front entrance and occupied an empty seat. Then she looked at me standing near the rear entrance and gestured to indicate that she would buy a ticket for me too. After that, she did not turn even once to look at me.

We hired an autorickshaw from the bus terminus. She looked very tired. Reclining in her seat, she laid the baby on her lap and closed her eyes, waking up only after we reached home. The house was in a horrible state. When the front door opened, an odious stench assaulted the nostrils. Barring a dim, fat bulb burning in the hall, the house was shrouded in darkness. Sulo set the baby down and switched on a few lights. A feeble voice called from inside. I was sure that it could not be Karunakaran's. Then, steering her wheelchair with effort, his wife came into the room. For a long time, she was unable to recognize me. After reminding her about me in several different ways, Sulo gave up trying. The family barber, who turned up from somewhere, led her away to another room. Afterwards, during my stay in that house, I saw her only twice. Since every inch of that house was covered by a thick layer of dust, I gathered that there was no one to take care of it. After laying her sleeping child on the bed, Sulo tidied up a portion of the hall in a listless manner. As though she had no wish to speak at all, she unpacked the food from the parcels in her bag, sent a portion to her mother, and then served me.

I presumed that Karunakaran was in no condition to eat. I could scarcely believe that I had come to the same house that I knew so well. I deluded myself that I was there for the first time, on Karunakaran's invitation and in compliance with the headmaster's instruction, and was waiting for him to arrive.

The bedroom adjoining the hall looked deserted. Through its wide-open doors wafted the smell of expired medicines. When I asked Sulo where her father was, she remained silent. Then, as if she thought that it was of no consequence, she told me that he was in the farmhouse. She herself ate just two idlis, as if she had little or no appetite. Later, with the help of a flashlight, we made our way to Karunakaran. Near the entrance of the farmhouse, their family barber was sitting on a string cot under a thatched-roof pandal. He scrambled to his feet when he saw us.

'How is Kavundar's health, Chinnappa?' Sulo asked as she pushed the slightly ajar door and swung it wide open. Unable to withstand the stench of decaying flesh emanating from inside, I held my breath and approached the bed. As soon as I saw Karunakaran's figure huddled under a blanket, my heart began to quiver. With a rag tied across her face to cover her nose and mouth, Sulo swept and tidied the room. Then she cleaned the deep sores on Karunakaran's buttocks painstakingly with warm water, applied an ointment, covered each sore with a Band-Aid and bandaged them. I supposed that it was one of her daily chores. Bracing myself, I even tried to help her.

'Bedsores,' Sulo explained in the impersonal tone of a doctor. I tried to work out why she had brought me here and why I had run into her now. In truth, there was nothing for me to do in that house. I assumed that the person who was steering this story of revenge had dragged me all the way and stationed me here only so I could see this dying man. 'Take care, Chinnappa. Call me if you need anything,' she said calmly to the barber and turned to leave. I followed her without a word. Pointing me to a folding cot in the veranda that looked very similar to the one used by the former vendor of used clothes, she went into her room with her baby and latched the door.

Gradually the house began to sink into an eerie silence. Unable to sleep, I kept tossing and turning for a long time. I wondered what might have happened to that former vendor of used clothes. I recalled the astringent taste of Sugandhi's last kiss. Was it truly over? My resolve to never see Sugandhi again—how long was it going to last? I, who had renounced everything forever and run away, was back again, for no good reason, in this house that seemed completely bereft of human presence, hiding like a ghoul in a corner of its dingy veranda.

After robbing me of all the wonderful moments of life and isolating me from it, this story of vengeance is moving rapidly towards a conclusion. Once it is over, will I become a nullity? Will there be nothing left for me to do or think about? I'll be roaming around as a body that no one cared about or as someone without even a body.

I was lost in these thoughts when Sulo's baby started crying. At first, I ignored it. I waited for some time, expecting Sulo to wake up. But there was no sign of that for a long time. The baby was screaming and bawling as though it was frightened. As if by involuntary reflex, I flung the blanket aside, got up and strode urgently, feet thudding, to Sulo's room, and knocked on the door. Just then, the baby stopped crying. I paused outside the door for a few seconds, not knowing what to do. Then I returned to my cot, covered myself with the blanket and hunkered down quietly. The next moment, just as I had expected, I heard the latch being drawn back. Sulo entered on tiptoe and turned on the light in the hall. I drew the blanket aside and sat up, pretending that I had just awakened and was looking at her in confusion. Sulo came straight to me.

'Was it you who knocked on my door just now?'

'No.' I was quick with my denial.

'It seemed like someone did. Did Chinnappa come here?'

I kept silent as though I did not know the answer to her question. She threw a suspicious glance at the entrance and the windows, and left. Then I heard a latch being drawn shut.

Oh god! What kind of man was I? Why did I lie just now, for no good reason? What was the problem in telling her the truth—that I had heard the baby's wails, thought that something was wrong and knocked on her door? Could a man fall lower than this? How much longer was Karunakaran going to survive in this house, spreading the unbearable stench of death? For some reason I believed that I couldn't recover from anything as long as Karunakaran was alive.

I could have killed him back then. But when I had the chance, I had done nothing despite being armed with a blood-soaked knife. Though there was sufficient privacy, time and opportunity, I let them slip away. Had I killed him then, fulfilling my vow of revenge, I wouldn't have experienced such a steep decline. I would have been an important figure in the annals of time. My testimony would have turned into a wonderful epic of valour. People crushed by oppression would have celebrated me as a hero. This tale of my revenge would have been adapted into a third-rate Tamil film or a cheap novel. Some itinerant singer with an udukkai—like Chellappa Pandithan or

Ramasami Pandaram—would have written the saga of this revenge as a string of ballads like the legend of Kunnadaiya Kavundan, filled them with his furious rhythms, and turned the nights of ordinary people intent on revelry into nights of terror. After being sentenced to death or imprisonment for life, I would have been sent to jail. I would have spent my life in a prison cell immersed in endless memories of the taste and fragrance of that wonderful first kiss from Sulo's pink-edged lips or, like the epic hero who kisses the hangman's rope, I would have ceased to exist. But this tale of vengeance that I began to write has been taken over by someone else. Karunakaran, who has been narrating this story from the other end, is emanating an unbearable stench from his putrid buttocks like some accursed celestial monarch. Whether it is visible from the outside or not, I too have decayed. Both of us have fallen into the same abyss. I have transformed into Karunakaran.

What was Sharada's role in this story? Might she be visualized as its centre, its origin or its body? Or was she no different from the insignificant characters in this story who knew nothing about the backdrop of any event—like my younger sister or Karunakaran's sickly wife who suffered from joint pains from the first to this final chapter? I was flummoxed. But why should Sulo, who was present in the story not because she was required but only because she was Karunakaran's daughter, and Sugandhi, who had no connection at all with any part of this story, be turned into sacrificial animals by this plot line? How essential was it for this story, scribbled on scraps of paper thirty years ago, that their lives had to be destroyed and they had to be forsaken and set adrift as betrayed women who could never heal themselves? How necessary was it for this banal story of vengeance to push Gowthaman, who had not fully outgrown his childish naivety, into a prison cell for the rest of his life? Who brought that pathetic creature, the vendor of used clothes, into this story? I supposed that I certainly had no part or responsibility in these developments. They were wrought by that other person who had hijacked the story from me. It was the result of my impotence in having let slip that extraordinary opportunity that had come my way.

Perhaps the opportunity I had now would be even better than the one I had missed. I wouldn't need to make any effort to wreak vengeance on this man who was without any protection and already almost dead. It would be easier than stepping on a worm or crushing a minuscule creature with no body. To incapacitate the lungs of this loan shark who was stubbornly drawing his last breaths and expel the life cowering in his ruthless and nearly moribund heart, a slight pressure with the back of one's hand on his thin rib cage, with its diseased, hollow bones in which the marrow had dried up, would be more than enough. If the denouement of this story was to be the death of that man called Karunakaran, it would end at that precise moment.

But what would I or anyone else gain from ending this story in a flash when it would have ended anyway in the natural course within the next few weeks, days or even minutes? It was possible, however, for me to retrieve this story from the cruel hands of that other person who was capriciously moving it along like a tyrant, with no semblance of a plot line, by using a few starkly prosaic sentences. I still had a chance to write the last sentence or, at the very least, the final word, of this already concluded story, whose ending had been secured so firmly that neither Karunakaran nor I, who had once started writing it from opposite ends, could intervene.

I got up. Carrying not even a small blunt knife or a flashlight or anything else, I walked on tiptoe towards that farmhouse enveloped by the odour of death where Karunakaran's life was hiding.

Should an unforeseen circumstance, or a startling or sensational incident, interfere with my decision, I had planned in advance how I would deal with it. What if Karunakaran got up from his bed? What if he began, unbelievably, to free himself from death's vicious hold? That other person could steer the narrative in any direction he chose, right? In that case, I had resolved to confront Karunakaran as a dreadful ghoul bent on revenge who would never retreat. From the burning pyre of time, I must grab this not wholly charred moment with its acrid smell and thrust it in his face. He should realize that the man who had been his obedient servant and trusted friend was, in fact, a vengeful snake who had been trailing his footsteps with cruel intent. At that moment of realization, his feeble heart might stop beating.

At the foot of the string cot under the pandal, I found Karunakaran's family barber lying prone. He must have been drunk out of his mind. Ignoring that pathetic creature, a distant relative who was crippled by feelings of inferiority because I would never grant him the privilege of kinship, I entered the house. As soon as I stepped into that room that reeked of death, I was taken aback. Screaming 'Aiyo!' or 'Oh god!', I bent down near Karunakaran, who had fallen off the bed and lay face down on the ground. If I had shouted 'Oh god!' then I might have intoned that phrase in a helpless situation for the first time in many years. The stench that rose from the crimson blood and pus oozing from his buttocks filled the whole room. In a state of either complete unconsciousness or total clarity, I tried to turn his putrid body over. Since his buttocks rubbed against the floor as he was being turned over, Karunakaran screamed in agony. Hearing the screams of one or both of us, Sulo arrived. I felt that something which had occurred a long time ago was happening again. I imagined Karunakaran as that former vendor of used clothes, and Sulo as Sugandhi, who was still struggling to recover from the intoxication of my illicit kisses. By now, Sulo was bent over her father's body. Both of us joined hands and tried to lift him. She was trembling. If I ignored the stench, it wouldn't be difficult for me to handle his weightless body on my own. I relieved Sulo and held him like a baby in both my arms. Sulo took a few minutes to straighten the bed and change the sheets with her pale, thin arms disfigured by bulging veins. After laying the dying body face down on the bed, I cleaned the pus and blood on my hands with a rag I found on the floor.

'God! ... Why don't you give me an injection or something and kill me! ... You will earn merit with that good deed,' Karunakaran groaned in a bitter voice he had never used before.

Sulo, who was trying to heat water on the stove to clean Karunakaran's sores or to prepare his medication, dropped the utensil with an alarming clang that matched the context. Then she crumbled, sat down where she stood and started crying. I dragged her to the wall and propped her against it.

I was transformed at once into someone who had to do everything, who dared not disobey the instructions of that other person, who was one of the weakest characters in this story. Boiling the water, cleaning and applying an ointment on the wounds, and stopping the bleeding by stuffing them with cotton, were the most urgent tasks. Next, I asked Sulo where the painkillers were kept, searched for them in the cupboard and gave Karunakaran a few. Then I waited for something to happen. After washing the blood and pus that had dripped all over the floor, sprinkling Dettol and cleaning the room, Sulo had gone to the kitchen. I thought she might come back with some fruit juice or milk. Karunakaran, who had begun to regain consciousness, opened his eyes very slowly—like a character in an animation film—and recognized me, the cartoon figure swaying before him. 'Clerk Sir, is it you?' He tried strenuously to raise his trembling hands and bring them together in greeting. 'May you stay healthy and prosperous all your life, Sir,' he blessed me. I was watching his tearful eyes with a weary smile. 'You never came home all these days…' he complained in a feeble voice. I did not respond to anything he said. Then he gazed at the roof in silence. 'Clerk Sir, is there anything to eat? I am hungry,' he said.

Sulo, who had entered the room just then, began to decant the fruit juice that she had brought in a jar into a porcelain cup. Karunakaran was observing our movements with his clouded eyes. Then he gestured for us to come closer. Assuming that the sign was addressed to both Sulo and me, I went to him with the cup of fruit juice.

'I don't want that, Sir. My taste buds are dead. Will you give me something hot and spicy? They think it will make the abscess swell up, so they refuse to give me anything. Even if I stick to a strict diet, how can I pull through at this stage? My body is festering already. Only two or three days, at the most.' Talking in a very faint voice, he raised his hand and tried to indicate the numbers using his fingers. Since the attempt failed, he let his hand drop to the side and, looking intently at me with his hazy eyes, asked me diffidently, 'I want a dosai. Just one dosai. Really craving it, Sir. Think of this as my final wish.' Then, in a manner that no one who knew him would have believed, he broke down and began to weep.

'I want to see my son, Sir. At any cost, arrange to bring him here on parole for two or three days at least, Sir. I'll die after seeing him with my own eyes,' he said.

As luck would have it, there was some dosai batter in the kitchen. With her eyes as still as a cadaver's, Sulo was trying to fulfil her father's final wish. She must be staying in her father's house most of the time, I thought. She must have broken off the relationship with her in-laws, at least for the time being. She never said anything about it, then or later. Very soon, the dosais, along with the coconut chutney that was Karunakaran's favourite item, were ready. Sulo was about to make Karunakaran lean on her chest like a child and feed him small pieces of the dosai, bit by bit. Then, as if ordained by fate, her child started crying. When I stood up to go and fetch the child, she stopped me with her eyes. I shifted Karunakaran's weight on to my shoulder and sent her away. Karunakaran ate eagerly. Tears had begun to flow from his eyes without restraint. After I washed his hands and laid him on the bed, he tried to grab my hands.

'Stay well, Sir. Why should I call you "Sir"? You are like a son to me; dearer than a son, in fact,' he gushed.

I was stunned. I realized that I could never bring this story under my control. Since I didn't want to go back to the bedroom, I sat on a chair under the thatched awning outside Karunakaran's farmhouse, smoking a cigarette. The family barber, who had fallen unconscious in his inebriated state, woke only at dawn.

The next day, Karunakaran's health had improved to a surprising extent. With the support of a crutch, he stood on his feet for a brief while. He ate two or three idlis in the morning and communicated his next craving to Sulo—chicken broth. He wanted to smoke as well. With Sulo's permission, I gave him a cigarette. She had foreseen her father's demise. Like an obedient and ever-grateful servant, I was ministering to the man on whom I had wanted to take revenge. Two days later, the family barber told me about Sulo. It was nothing surprising or unexpected. There was no chance of a reconciliation between her and her husband, of her living with him ever again. He also told me that she had filed for divorce in the family court. When I heard this, I was inwardly happy. I couldn't say whether it was out of love or a feeling of revenge. But I couldn't discern any change in the way Sulo treated me. She kept talking to me in a peremptory and disrespectful tone. In a way, I had begun to enjoy it. I was taking liberties with her and trying to normalize it through cheeky and humorous banter. Assuming that the household was now entirely in my control, I tried to fulfil Karunakaran's final wishes. During our chat late one night, the family barber mentioned in passing that among the people of this town who were keenly monitoring my movements, salacious rumours were circulating about my relationship with the household. The barbed looks of people I happened to meet in the bazaar and the bus station were thrilling to me. I observed the flame of jealousy blazing in many pairs of eyes. At Sulo's request, I went to the bank, withdrew some money and gave it to her; then I set out for a meeting with the lawyer. I went to my office and told the supervisor that since a close relative was on his deathbed, I needed ten days' leave, and got it sanctioned.

'Did anyone come to see me, Sir?' I asked the supervisor as I was leaving. I thought Sugandhi might have come and inquired about me. He said no one had turned up. Then I checked with the office watchman and another clerk who was close to me and confirmed what the supervisor had told me. Hugely disappointed, I came out of the office. I thought to myself that it was certainly good for me as well as that former vendor of used clothes. I didn't quite know what good might await a man like me who had dropped everything abruptly and run away without a word to anyone. While travelling in an autorickshaw to the lawyer's house, I suddenly remembered the old M-80 moped that I had abandoned. I wondered whether I should go home, pick it up and take it to a mechanic. By the time I reached the lawyer's house, however, I had dropped the idea and started thinking about Gowthaman's parole application. After an inordinately long wait, I was finally summoned to the lawyer's desk. The lawyer understood the issue in no time. 'It won't be all that difficult,' he said. He gave me a form and asked me to come back after getting a few signatures from Karunakaran's wife and the doctor.

'But it will take two or three days. Is that all right?' he said.

'What else can we do, Sir?'

'Will he survive until then?' he asked, and promised to arrange for Gowthaman's parole as early as possible.

When I returned home after midnight, Sulo was waiting for me. Over dinner, I told her about my meeting with the lawyer. Even at that late hour, she went to her mother and came back with the old woman's thumbprint on the form. She woke up early in the morning and came with me to meet the doctor. She sat with her child on the pillion of their TVS-50, which was still in good condition. I noticed that many people were watching us with wonder and dismay. A kind of joy had begun to fill my heart. I thought it inevitable that this story of revenge would turn into a love story in its final phase. Whether the ending was absurd or not could be determined only later. Sulo seemed completely unperturbed. While she was sitting on the moped as well as at other moments, whenever her body grazed against mine, she behaved as though she was not conscious of it at all.

Her tears had dried up. She behaved as if she was through with life and there was nothing to be gained from living any more. But late at night, after returning from court, when I told her that Gowthaman had been granted parole and would be brought home in a couple of days, she was terribly upset. 'I don't know if Appa will be alive when Annan comes home,' she said, adding that her father's pulse was getting weaker. As always, I listened to her in silence. Then she said with a sigh, 'It will be good for him if he is dead by then. Dying would be far better than watching his beloved son stand before him in handcuffs.' I had never imagined that she could fall apart in this way. We were sitting opposite each other in Karunakaran's old office room. While I was stuck in a reverie, immersed in the memory of that first pink-edged kiss I had received from her, she leaned on my shoulder. 'What will I do now, 'pa?' She broke down and began to cry. With extreme diffidence and an intolerable sense of guilt, I took her in my arms. Her hard breasts dissolved in a flash and began to fill me up like a warm liquid. I lifted her tear-streaked face and placed a gentle kiss on those lips which tasted of seawater. She trembled. Something was brewing. But before we could put a finger on it, she broke free and disappeared.

However, just like the first kiss I had received from her—in the same room, but under circumstances that were the exact opposite of the present—this one, too, proved meaningless. Sulo forged an unbelievable compromise with her husband's family when they came to offer condolences after Karunakaran's demise. With Karunakaran's dead body as a witness, negotiations for a settlement were held under the direction of an elderly relative who had accompanied them. Watching the proceedings from a distance, I tried and failed to catch Sulo's eye. But she looked at me later for one last time. Unable to make any sense of her intense gaze that pierced right through my heart, I stepped out of the house for the last time.

No one who saw Gowthaman, released on parole and brought in with his hands bound, was able to bear the grief of that sight. Women paused their wailing to take in the scene in silence.

Gowthaman falling at the feet of Sulo's husband for her sake was something that no one had anticipated. As if they had been waiting only for that turn of events, everyone changed their stance in great haste. Cutting through the crowd, the elderly relative made his way to Gowthaman and raised him to his feet. As happens in the final scene of an emotional drama, everyone submitted to the old man's command. It was at that moment that I turned into a character of no importance in this story. The ceremonies were over and everyone was taking their leave. Sulo's mother-in-law, who had assumed responsibility for all matters, was busy settling accounts with various parties. As if my place in the scheme of things was already clear, I was standing apart next to the family barber under a pandal that had been freshly erected with green coconut fronds. Then, hearing someone call me, I went over and stood before them tentatively, like a cartoon character. Sulo, who had turned suddenly into a black-and-white photograph, was talking to her brother. Her mother-in-law had taken Sulo's extremely tired child on her lap. When I presented myself, she stared at me with her bitter eyes.

Gowthaman had recovered. Clad in the brand-new white dhoti which had been given to him for his father's final rites, he was sitting on a wooden chair. He got up as soon as he saw me. Taking me by the hand, he made me sit on a plastic chair that lay vacant before him. As he expressed his gratitude for the services I had rendered to Karunakaran, I was taken by surprise at the dignity and self-confidence evident in his tone. He was concise, clear and attentive, as though he was reading out a resolution. Others in the vicinity were listening keenly to his words. It seemed like an event held to mark the completion of a ritual. When I stood at the entrance, waiting to take my leave, Sulo's husband rushed out and started telling me something in a low whisper. I couldn't hear a word of what he was saying. It was then that, from a secret spot a short distance away, Sulo's deep gaze bored into me with deliberate intent; then it passed me without betraying any emotion.

But two days earlier, when Karunakaran was still alive, Sharada had brought this story to a conclusion. She was able to seize this story of vengeance that had belonged entirely to her, from that other person who was steering it in any direction he pleased, and bring it to a conclusion with a most ruthless sentence.

When I was in the office room, still brooding about that kiss from Sulo which tasted like seawater, there was a call from Sharada that felt like it was the next sentence in this story. She was livid.

'I knew it when I didn't hear from you for the past fifteen days. What are you doing there? Have you resumed your love drama again?'

Then I told her everything in a calm voice. By 'everything' I meant up to the point where Karunakaran was on his deathbed. Then she told me about her wish to see him. I promised to call her as soon as he breathed his last; she was quiet for some time.

'How is he now?'

'Like I told you. He may not survive another couple of days.'

'Is he able to speak?'

'Hmm.'

'Is he in a condition to understand if something is told to him?'

'Hmm.'

'Did you tell him anything?'

'…'

'Weren't you going to confess everything to him, even about the letter that you wrote?' Her voice turned hoarse. The rage within emerged as a sarcastic laugh. 'All right, then. I'll come by in the morning. Stay right there,' she said and disconnected the call. As if under a curse, I waited for her through the night without a wink of sleep. Then, just before sunrise, I leaned back awkwardly in that wooden chair and fell asleep. When Sulo roused me awake to say that Sharada had come to see me, I sat up bewildered, as though I had just recovered from a nightmare. I splashed some water on my face and came to the veranda. Sharada was looking at Karunakaran's family photographs which had been framed and hung on the walls. She looked flustered. I stood before her like a culprit who had given himself up. With her brown eyes, Sharada was subjecting the photographs, mounted in a chronological sequence at a height of more than six feet, to intense scrutiny. Sulo took it as an expression of childlike curiosity. She even tried to offer Sharada a commentary on the photographs, saying in a casual and friendly tone, 'Who knows when these photographs were taken! We weren't even born then.'

Then, in a move that surprised both of us, Sharada lifted her hands in an apparent attempt to remove a photograph from the wall. Watching her, Sulo set the coffee cup down on the table. 'Wait,' she told Sharada, then climbed on to a chair, took the photograph off the nail and handed it to Sharada, who seemed to be on edge as she received it. I was still clueless when she pointed to each person in the photograph and asked Sulo who they were. When I noticed that her lips were trembling, her breathing had become uneven, and beads of sweat had begun to appear on her forehead and the nape of her neck, I could only think cruelly to myself, 'After all, wasn't he the first man to kiss her?'

Sharada drank her coffee in a hurry. Then she cast a compassionate look at Sulo's face and asked, 'Where is your father now?' When Sulo came forward to lead Sharada to Karunakaran, I stopped her and accompanied Sharada. As soon as we neared Karunakaran's room, Sharada, who was walking purposefully ahead of me, stopped me at the entrance and entered the room alone. My whole body had begun to tremble. I could no longer evade the crisis of coming face to face with the final chapter of this story of vengeance and the climactic moment that I had been anticipating for a very long time. Sharada came back in no time, as swiftly as she had entered the room. Her face had cracked. Those brown eyes were nearly dead. I thought she might have found the stench in Karunakaran's room unbearable and rushed out. But then, she also wanted to leave right away.

'Please stay. You can go home after having tiffin with us. It will only take five minutes,' Sulo said as she drew up a chair for Sharada. Ignoring her request, Sharada crossed the doorstep and waited for me outside. I made her sit on the moped and rode with her to the bus stop. I thought she might say something after she had calmed down. She sat in silence until the end, not saying a word. Once she got down from the vehicle after we reached the bus stop, she stood with her now ashen eyes downcast, staring at the ground, like someone who had done something terribly wrong. Then, with only seconds to go before the bus arrived, she lifted her head and looked at me.

Knowing that she was going to say something important, I tried to guess what it might be. She told me with great diffidence, in a hushed tone, 'This is not that man. He is someone else. Yes, both had the same name, Karunakaran, and since their appearance also seemed to match, you made a mistake.'

After blurting out in a hurry what seemed like a very ordinary sentence and in no mood to even say goodbye, she boarded the bus that almost grazed her as it came to a halt.

Translator's Note

'We are all recovering children'
HANIF KUREISHI

THE URGE TO TAKE REVENGE and inflict punishment is as old as humanity. It's a recurring theme in the myths and epics of ancient cultures. While the pursuit of vengeance is seen as a noble quest for justice, its destructive consequences are also acknowledged as inescapable. Panchali's vow to avenge her disrobing in the court of the Kauravas culminates in the eighteen-day war in Kurukshetra in the Mahabharatham. In the Old Testament, Absalom's revenge on his half-brother Amnon for the rape of Tamar, his sister, sets off a chain of tragic events which ends with Absalom being slain on the battlefield. Greek mythology is awash with tales of bloody revenge, with Nemesis, the goddess of retribution for evil deeds and undeserved good fortune, restoring the balance between good and evil.

For a modern individual, the private journey towards revenge presents a difficult and complex terrain that they must navigate within and without. Life is an endless source of second chances, and a reductive obsession with seeking vengeance for a specific event in the past is irrational and unhealthy. It is also a quest circumscribed by practical constraints: feasibility, laws of the land and fear of retaliation. In our contemporary world, 'getting even' can be both risky and dangerous.

From a more enlightened perspective, the quest for revenge can also be morally ambivalent, resulting at all times in a needless escalation of human suffering. In the sage words of Mahatma Gandhi, 'An eye for an eye makes the whole world blind.' Yet we see nations and individuals alike muddling their way towards flawed visions of retributive justice, leaving horror and destruction in their wake.

The protagonist of *The Solitude of a Shadow*, Devibharathi's first novel to be translated into English, is suddenly overtaken by a hitherto dormant urge to wreak vengeance upon a man who had molested his sister and abused him thirty years ago. It describes with painful clarity the poverty and isolation of inhabiting an obsession, a shadowy existence, when life itself—wild, fecund and unruly—flourishes all around the protagonist.

The Solitude of a Shadow is also a narrative of our society, with its overlapping hierarchies of caste, wealth and power. Through a fevered first-person narrative rendered in clear, sharp sentences, Devibharathi shows us how treacherous and illusory our hunger for personal retribution can become, and how our search for redress can lead us into a zone of desolation where we are left alone with our frailties and dark impulses, with unavoidably tragic consequences. From a societal perspective, the novel is also an astutely observed document of the politics and social relations within a community living in an impoverished and poorly endowed region in western Tamil Nadu.

Nizhalin Thanimai (2012), the Tamil original of *The Solitude of a Shadow,* is the second work of this author to be published in my translation. Earlier, I had translated a collection of his short stories as *Farewell, Mahatma* (2014). The language and storytelling style of the stories were distinctive and completely modern; in a sense, they were the key to the author's vision as a writer.

'I wanted to explore the meaning of life through language. Though these experiences are not from my own life, I wanted to understand life as it exists,' Devibharathi had told an interviewer at the time. His language was certainly a departure from the standard Tamil of the early pioneers and the regional dialect of the subalterns who came later.

As someone who began his literary journey in the early 1980s, Devibharathi was an early adopter of the secular prose style of the modernists. His approach to narrative language eschews special emphasis on the anthropological-ethnographic dimension, because he feels that it accentuates the existing differences between communities and reifies them in a way. His diction, even in dialogue, is simple, formal and direct. His portrayal of the material circumstances as well as the interiority of the characters is stark and clear-eyed, without recourse to the conventional tropes of Tamil fiction or the grammar of role-play that is so pervasive in our culture. His grasp of atmosphere, both natural and man-made, is never less than sharp and edgy. His incisive yet nuanced portrayal of the relentless dynamic of power relations between human beings can be overwhelming at times. He uses the novel format to spring surprises at every turn, switching seamlessly between rural and urban settings, between the present and the past, and between reality and fantasy. Always keeping his narrative taut, he presents the unfolding destinies of his characters as essentially mysterious, something the reader must make sense of on their own.

As a translator, it has been my attempt to make these distinctive qualities come alive in a new language. It was a pleasure translating this superb novel—its language, flow and craft. I hope the reader will derive as much pleasure in experiencing them on their own.

Finally, I would like to thank Arpita Basu for her fine editing of the manuscript, Rinita Banerjee for doing a splendid job with the proofs, and Rahul Soni for his support and guidance in the publication of the book in its present form.

N. Kalyan Raman
1 January 2024

About the Author

Devibharathi (b. 1957) was born and raised in a small village in western Tamil Nadu, the second of five children in a schoolmaster's family. He has worked as a political activist, government employee, journalist, managing editor of a leading literary magazine, and scriptwriter for television programmes. During a writing career spanning more than forty years, Devibharathi has published two collections of short stories, two novellas, four novels, a play, and two non-fiction anthologies containing essays and memoirs. *Farewell, Mahatma*, a collection of short stories in English translation, was published in 2014. *Nizhalin Thanimai*, the original of *The Solitude of a Shadow*, is his first novel. His fiction has received wide attention and praise from Tamil readers and critics. He has received several awards, including the inaugural Tannaram Literary Award in 2021, and the Kalaignar Porkizhi and Sahitya Akademi awards in 2023. He lives and works in a village in Tamil Nadu's Tiruppur district.

About the Translator

N. Kalyan Raman is a translator of contemporary Tamil fiction and poetry into English. Over the past twenty-five years, he has published translations of fourteen works of Tamil fiction by important writers such as Ashokamitran, Poomani, Devibharathi, Perumal Murugan, Vaasanthi and Salma. His translations of contemporary Tamil poets have been published widely in journals and anthologies in India and abroad. Kalyan Raman also writes on cinema, politics and literature for leading journals and magazines in India. His translation of Perumal Murugan's *Poonachi* was shortlisted for the inaugural JCB Prize (2018), and longlisted for the National Book Award for Translated Literature (2020) and Sahitya Akademi's Translation Prize – English (2022). In 2017, he received the prestigious Pudumaipithan Award for his contribution to the cause of Tamil literature through his translations. He lives and works in Chennai.

HarperCollins *Publishers* India

At HarperCollins India, we believe in telling the best stories and finding the widest readership for our books in every format possible. We started publishing in 1992; a great deal has changed since then, but what has remained constant is the passion with which our authors write their books, the love with which readers receive them, and the sheer joy and excitement that we as publishers feel in being a part of the publishing process.

Over the years, we've had the pleasure of publishing some of the finest writing from the subcontinent and around the world, including several award-winning titles and some of the biggest bestsellers in India's publishing history. But nothing has meant more to us than the fact that millions of people have read the books we published, and that somewhere, a book of ours might have made a difference.

As we look to the future, we go back to that one word—a word which has been a driving force for us all these years.

Read.

Harper Collins

4th

HARPER PERENNIAL

HARPER BUSINESS

HARPER BLACK

हार्पर हिन्दी

HarperCollins *Children'sBooks*

HARPER DESIGN

HARPER VANTAGE

Harper Sport